ENTICE

Marie Tuhart

https://www.marietuhart.com/

ENTICE

When Crystal Hayen walks into Jordan Frost's office, sparks fly. The spunky paralegal captured his attention the first time they met in more ways than one. Crystal is perfect for the job he needs to have done. But he wants more. He wants all Crystal can give him. He only hopes she's up to the challenge.

Crystal's attraction to Jordan is immediate and powerful. But she's vowed never to date a co-worker again. Worse yet, he'll be her boss. She's already lost one job due to to a personal relationship; she won't do it it again. When Jordan agrees to an ironclad contract between them that her job is safe, Crystal finds herself free to explore a world that has intrigued her for a long time, but old fears haunt her.

Crystal and Jordan are thrown together while working the case. The stakes increase and threaten to spill over into their private lives and the lives of their friends. While both have secrets, their past and present collide. They must confront old attitudes and beliefs in order to open their hearts to each other and find a lasting future together.

Dedication

This book wouldn't have happened without the following people:

Laurie, thank you for all your expertise editing and formatting.

Nia and Isabel, my critique partners, who always find ways for me to improve my story.

Red Quill Editing, your editing is the best.

To My Readers:

This book contains elements of the BDSM lifestyle that are only true to life in this book. There are varying forms of the lifestyle as decided between the people involved. While I researched and talked with people in the lifestyle, this is my take on how my characters choose to live.

If you decide to explore the lifestyle yourself, please remember to always be safe. Never go home with someone you don't know. Attend a munch or a small get-together first to see if this is something you want in your life. Reading about the lifestyle and living it are very different.

Any liberties taken with the lawyers or the law in this book is this author's voice. I researched as much as possible, and many things are based on the law in the state where the book is based.

There is no mention of the coronavirus that exists in our world right now. I purposely left it out. This is a place for you to escape.

Chapter One

Crystal Hayden strode with confidence into the office of Frost and Company, Attorneys at Law, in Pleasant Valley. The firm was looking for a paralegal, and as a freelance paralegal, she had the freedom to take jobs when and with the firms she wanted.

She needed a job, but she *wanted* this job, in particular. The grapevine said this firm was handling a huge case, and if the courts ruled in their client's favor, it could set far-reaching legal precedents. The case could also make the firm a household name and, by association, further her career. So, after talking to people in the know, she set up an interview.

Crystal stepped into the lobby of the building, the warm air caressing her cool skin. She removed her raincoat as she waited for the elevator. It had decided to rain in the Pacific Northwest today, nothing odd there. The wet weather was part of living here, and she'd rather live here than anywhere else.

The elevator pinged, and Crystal stepped in and pushed the button for the third floor. The firm occupied the entire floor. When she stepped out, her feet sank into plush, likely very expensive beige carpet as she made her way to the reception area. Very nice. Top end leather furniture. Chrome with beveled glass on the cocktail and end tables, an espresso machine, real china for coffee, and what looked like Waterford crystal glasses for the bottled water in the small refrigerator next to the coffee station.

The muted chatter of the law office made her smile. She sometimes missed the camaraderie an office setting offered. She stepped up to the curved receptionist desk. The young woman smiled back, her strawberry-blonde hair caressing her shoulders, her blue eyes sparkling.

"Good morning, welcome to the Frost law offices. How may I help you?"

"I'm Crystal Hayden. I'm here to meet with Kendra Winslow about the paralegal job."

"Oh yes. If you'll have a seat, I'll let Ms. Winslow know you're here." Her gaze moved to the coat over Crystal's arm. "If you'd like, I can hang your coat up."

"Yes, thank you." Crystal carefully handed the young woman her raincoat.

"Please feel free to have coffee or water."

"Thank you." Crystal wandered over to the waiting area. Drinking anything was out of the question right now. Why was she so nervous? She'd been on interviews before. Crystal glanced down at her outfit. Everything still in place.

"Ms. Hayden," a soft voice said.

Crystal raised her head to the older woman standing in front of her. "Yes."

"Kendra Winslow." She held her hand out. Kendra had on a navy pantsuit with a white blouse tailored to fit her perfectly.

"Ms. Winslow." Crystal clasped the office manager's hand.

"Kendra, please. If you'll follow me." Kendra moved down the hallway.

Crystal followed, noting the soft painted walls and original artwork. No lithographs or prints. Oil on canvas. Kendra gestured for Crystal to enter the small conference room.

"Please have a seat," Kendra said as she shut the door. "Is it still cold and windy outside?"

Crystal pushed a strand of stray hair back. "Yes, Western Washington in winter is always a surprise."

"At least it's not snowing," Kendra said, taking the chair to Crystal's left at the circular table, leaving the one to the right empty. "Thank you for coming in on such short notice."

"Not a problem. I was surprised to see the firm needed a short-term paralegal." Surprised, but grateful. She needed a challenge.

"Yes." Kendra opened the file she'd brought in with her. "Your references are impeccable, along with your reputation."

"Thank you." She didn't know what else to say. A knock sounded at the door.

"That would be Mr. Frost. He wanted to sit in. Come in."

Frost. The name tingled at the back of her neck. While she'd done her research, she... How could she have missed it? There was only one name: Jordan. She closed her eyes.

"Good morning, Kendra." Then his brown gaze turned to her. "Crystal."

"You two know each other?" Kendra asked as Jordan took the chair to Crystal's right.

Damn it, why hadn't she'd put two and two

together? She trembled. She and her friends, Sierra and Tess, had discussed their jobs over coffee a little over a month ago.

"Crystal and I have met, yes."

He leaned forward, and she caught a whiff of his cologne. A woodsy scent that reminded her of hiking in the forest. *Mind on the interview.*

"I wish you would have told me," Kendra said.

"My apologies, Kendra," Jordan replied. "The meeting was over a month ago, and it was coffee with mutual friends."

"Very well." Kendra looked back down at the papers in front of her. "As I was saying, your references are stellar, as is your resume."

"Thank you."

Jordan's intense stare sent a wave of uneasiness through Crystal's body. Damn that heat. She shouldn't have worn a suit jacket today.

Jordan shifted in his seat. "Why do you want this job, Crystal?" he asked.

The husky tone of his voice sent a tingle of awareness down her spine. She was a mass of contradiction. First unease, now awareness. *He's a lawyer and your potential boss*, she reminded herself. She wouldn't get involved with a lawyer, not again.

"The grapevine made it sound like a challenge." The ad hadn't said much. *Paralegal wanted. Experience with civil law a plus. Temporary position for three months, possibly less.*

"The grapevine?" He shook his head. "Figures. I knew I wouldn't be able to keep this completely quiet. And yes, it will be a challenge." He leaned back in his chair.

"It was bound to get out," Kendra said, then looked at Crystal. "The case is very sensitive. So you'll understand there are some legalities we need to work out. Are you and Jordan going to have any issues?"

"We won't." Crystal's voice was firm. Kendra looked at Jordan.

"Kendra, will you give us a minute?"

Crystal saw the surprise on Kendra's face, but she nodded and left the room. Crystal kept her gaze on Jordan. He was watching her, and she had to force herself not to shift under his scrutiny.

"I'll ask Kendra to come back in a minute. I wanted to make sure you're okay working closely with me. You were pretty upset with me after coffee."

Crystal looked down at her hands. She was a professional, and this was the office, not a coffee shop. Yeah, she'd been a bit curt with him. She blamed it on two parents arguing and their little boy looking so upset. How many times in her childhood had an argument like that turned into a punishment?

"I was upset. I shouldn't have taken it out on you. I apologize."

"I can understand why it upset you. I dislike when parents air their issues in front of their kids, and I accept your apology." He rubbed his chin. "I want to make this clear. You'll be working for me, exclusively."

A tremor went through her body. The way he said it made her think of late nights and midnight kisses. "What about the other lawyers?" Thank goodness her voice was steady because her body was reacting to Jordan in ways it shouldn't be.

"They have their own paralegals." Jordan leaned forward, his expression serious. "I asked around when you made the appointment, Crystal. You're one of the best paralegals in the field. I need someone like you."

He'd checked her out; she hadn't expected any less. Maybe next time she'd do better due diligence when researching the lawyers in the firm before agreeing to the interview. "What is the case?"

"Let me call Kendra back in." Jordan stood and went to the door. Kendra stood there, her arms crossed over her chest.

"Inappropriate," Kendra said as she walked past Jordan and back into the room. Crystal's gut clenched. Maybe she should leave and look elsewhere. But she didn't want to. This case sounded like something interesting, and Crystal couldn't wait to do research.

Kendra sat down. She glared at Jordan as he retook his seat, then looked at Crystal and blew out a breath. Crystal steadied herself.

"Maybe it would be better if I turn the job down," she said. The last thing she wanted was to make an enemy of the operations manager.

Kendra's green eyes lit up with surprise. "I was pointing out to Jordan that he wasn't acting in the firm's best interest in asking me to leave." Kendra took a breath. "It's not your fault or mine. Jordan has a tendency to be hands-on in certain things. I'm trying to break him of the habit."

Jordan flashed a grin. "I wanted to clear the air with Crystal. She asked me about the case, which is why I called you back in. All I can say is it's a civil case. I can't go into particulars until we have a signed contract and NDA in place."

Crystal's spine stiffened. "An NDA?" While nondisclosure agreements in the legal profession weren't unheard of, her gut tensed. She was still wary of them in the workplace.

"Yes, this case is sensitive." Jordan's gaze focused in on her.

"I see." She shifted in her seat. Sensitive. The word didn't make her think of the case. A shiver ran over her skin. Why was she reacting to Jordan this way? It was like she'd never been attracted to someone before. Crystal took a deep breath and pushed her fascination aside. "The ad mentioned this is a temporary assignment for three months?"

"That is correct," Kendra said, flipping the papers in the folder.

"We have depositions set up a week from today, with a hearing a week after, so you're going to have your work cut out for you, getting up to speed." Jordan spread his hands on the table.

"Why did you wait so long to hire someone?" Another anomaly.

Kendra chuckled. "Because he thought he could handle it himself when his paralegal went out on maternity leave."

"There is that." Jordan's finger tapped against the table. "Also because I didn't think the case would get this far." He ran his hand over the back of his neck. "I'm in a bind. I hear you're the best. I'm willing to pay for your expertise and time." He named a salary.

Kendra rolled her eyes, and Crystal's jaw dropped.

"You have to be kidding." He had to be. She was prepared to negotiate a fair wage, but doing so would be moot. Yes, she was at the top of her field, but seriously… She shook her head.

"I'm not kidding. You're the best. You're not afraid of hard work or long hours. Your research skills are the stuff of legend. This salary takes everything into account."

"It's far too much."

"I've never had anyone tell me I was paying them too much." The humor in his voice was apparent.

"It's definitely a first for me as well," Kendra said.

Crystal shrugged. "Being truthful."

"As am I. You're worth the money."

A tremor wracked her body at his husky tone. What was it about his voice? "All right. May I see the employment agreement?" She looked at Kendra.

"Of course." Kendra pulled it out of the folder and passed it to her.

Crystal began reading. "Sure of me, were you?" He already had her name and certification details filled in.

"Jordan prepared it; it's my job, but he overruled me," Kendra said.

"I was being hopeful." He grinned at her.

His grin sent a tingle of awareness all the way to her toes. *He's a lawyer; don't fall for his charm.* The employment agreement was standard. Crystal was still concerned about the money. She had never argued before about someone paying her too much. "The NDA?"

More papers were passed across the table. Crystal read it.

Most of it was standard, but there were a few areas of concern.

"I can't discuss the case with anyone at all?" A bit unusual. Well, not exactly. She never talked about an active case with anyone, not even her best friends.

"I have a list of professionals you can talk with about the case and, of course, our client and those here in the office who need to know, but no one else."

Crystal nodded. "What about the clause: *There will be disclosures and other information pertaining to this case you may find personally offensive and/or disturbing.* What kind of case is this?" The hair on the back of her neck stood up.

"Civil case. I can't say more about it at this point." Jordan sat back in his seat.

She placed the papers on the table. "I understand your client's desire to ensure their privacy, but I need to know more before I sign anything so I can make an informed decision."

Jordan stared at her with those mesmerizing brown eyes. "How about this? Sign the NDA, and I'll explain. Then, if you don't want to work on the case, no harm, no foul." He glanced at Kendra.

"I can agree to that," Kendra said.

Crystal frowned. This was highly unusual. Her fingers twitched. What harm could there be in signing the NDA and finding out what the case was about?

Jordan's phone rang, and she jumped in her seat. She hadn't realized how quiet the room was.

"Excuse me, I need to take this." He stood up and went to the opposite side of the room.

Crystal nodded and began reading the NDA once more.

"I know this is unusual, but this is an unusual case," Kendra said.

Crystal was about to answer when she heard Jordan speak. "Sage, I know." Jordan's voice was soft.

"I'm working on it. You have to trust me. If you and Brady are seen together, it will spell trouble." He paused. "Yes, I know you miss him, and he wants to be with you."

Crystal glanced up to see the frustration on Jordan's face. Whatever the client was saying was not making him happy.

"The first court date is soon. Just hold on. Okay?" His features lightened. "Thank you. Yes, see you Thursday." He ended the call and looked at Crystal. "Sorry."

"Clients come first." What an intriguing conversation. And if it was tied to the case he wanted her working on, decision made. She picked up the pen lying on the table between her and Kendra and signed the NDA, then slid the document over to Kendra. "Now tell me about this case."

Kendra picked it up and nodded. "My client has been accused of abuse," Jordan said.

"Wouldn't that be criminal?"

"Yes, my client was arrested and charged, but then the DA dropped the charges. This is a civil case. His family is making the allegations."

"The accused is a woman?" Her eyes widened in surprise. Unusual, but it happened.

"My client is a woman. Everything that happened between my client and her su…boyfriend was consensual."

He'd stumbled over a word. Crystal wondered who the client was. "There's something you're not telling me."

"This is a very delicate situation."

"And that's my cue." Kendra stood up. "Jordan

will explain what he needs to and call me back in when you're ready to go over the employment contract."

"Thank you, Kendra," Jordan said.

Crystal watched the woman leave, but before she closed the door, Kendra gave Jordan a hard look.

"I know you're friends with Sierra," Jordan said the minute the door closed. "How much has she told you about her and Max?"

"Probably everything. She and Max… Oh." The light bulb came on. "This involves someone in the kink community."

"Yes. I wasn't sure how much Sierra had shared."

"Only about how she's Max's submissive and how much she enjoys him dominating her." Crystal suppressed a tremor of fear mixed with excitement. Her sensuality had been suppressed as a teenager. College had helped her come out of her shell, but there were times she could still feel the beatings at the hand of her father.

"Do you understand Dominance and submission?"

"A little bit." Crystal shifted in her chair again. Jordan's eyes followed her movement. A gleam lit his gaze, and she forced herself to still. Of all the things she had thought they'd talk about, this was not one of them. Was Jordan a Dom? Her body heated. Whoa, time to pull those thoughts back and remind herself: She didn't date lawyers.

"Before I go on about this case in particular, how much do you understand about kink?" He leaned forward in his chair and settled his elbows on the table.

She froze in her seat. How to answer? She'd talked with Sierra, but they hadn't gone into details.

"I've read about it in romance books and from some of the things Sierra has told me."

"No practical experience?"

"Not really." If her parents even thought she had what they considered 'impure thoughts', they'd punish her and put her in the sin room for days. And then there were the men she'd dated. They'd tried a club and some bondage, but it wasn't anything like what Sierra had told her.

Jordan leaned forward, his hands splayed out on the table. Her gaze was captured by his. Her heart rate picked up at the smoldering look in his brown eyes.

"I need a paralegal who is open to doing the necessary research, which will likely include talking with others in the kink community."

"I can do that." Crystal forced herself to breathe normally. Jordan was too close. Just like the night at the book club meeting and again at the coffee shop, his heat, his masculinity, called out to her. Her fingers tangled together in her lap.

"Can you?" He turned his hands palms up. "It means we're going to be working closely together. Late nights and weekends."

Crystal swallowed. How was she going to handle her attraction to him? She blew out a breath. "I can be professional; can you?" She almost clamped her hand over her mouth. She hadn't meant for those words to slip out.

Jordan's eyes widened, and then a grin spread over his lips.

"That came out wrong. You're going to be my boss and nothing more." She closed her eyes. She was making a mess of this. "What I mean is—"

"I know what you meant. I'm going to lay my cards on the table, so to speak. I'm attracted to you, Crystal. There was a spark from the first night." He held his hand up when she opened her mouth. "Please, let me finish. I will be professional on the job, totally and completely."

"Jordan, if you're going to be my boss, we can't have a personal relationship." Oh but she wanted to. Where was her willpower? He was a lawyer, and she'd promised herself—after her last failed relationship with a lawyer—she would never get involved with anyone she worked with.

"This has nothing to do with your job and never will."

"I want that in the employment contract." The words came out before she could stop them.

His grin widened. "Done." He stood. "Be right back." Crystal blinked. What the hell happened? Before she could analyze it, Jordan returned with Kendra.

Kendra had a stack of papers in her hand. "Here's the new employment contract," Kendra said, sliding it across to Crystal.

She flipped through the pages until she got to the end. She read the added wording. *Oh my, he's serious.* He'd put in the contract anything personal between them had nothing to do with her job, and she would be paid in full no matter what. Even if she left the job early.

"Change the 'paid in full no matter what' to 'paid in full for all work completed at the time of separation'." Crystal pushed the contract back to Kendra.

Kendra made the changes, initialed, as did Jordan, then gave it back to Crystal who initialed it. She read the rest and then picked up a pen. This was crazy.

She was crazy.

"Hold on," Kendra said. "Let's get a notary up here. I want this done properly."

"Agreed." Jordan pulled his phone out.

"Hey, Holly, it's Jordan. Can you come up to the office, conference room one for a minute and notarize a contract? Thanks." He hung the phone up. "Holly will be here in a few minutes."

She hadn't expected the notary, but it would protect her and his firm. She reached down and pulled her wallet out of her bag and then pulled out her driver's license. When there was a knock on the door, Crystal straightened.

Jordan opened the door, and a bubbly blonde woman walked in. "Okay, Jordan, what do you need?"

"I want you to notarize an employment contract between myself and Crystal."

The woman looked at her and smiled. "Easy job." She sat down at the table and laid down her book and seal. "The contract please, Jordan, and Crystal, your ID. We'll get this taken care of."

Crystal handed Holly her license.

"Very good." She handed them back and then flipped to the last page of the contract. "All right, if you'll each sign."

Crystal took the pen Holly held out, signed the contract, and handed it to Jordan, and he signed. Holly signed and applied the raised seal. "Done." She left the office.

"I'll get you copies of this and the NDA for your records." Kendra stood and took the papers off the table. "Be right back."

"Now that's out of the way…" He gestured for

her to sit.

Crystal shook her head as she put her license away and sat down. "You're moving fast."

"Time's of the essence. Can you start tomorrow?"

"Yes." Her fingers tingled with excitement to start a new job.

"Good. I start at seven, but if you're here by eight, it will be fine. Tomorrow I have to be in court in the morning. Kendra is usually here by seven-thirty, and Valerie, the receptionist, arrives at eight."

"I can be here when Valerie gets here." She ran over her schedule in her head.

"Works for me. There's an office next to mine; I've had a desk installed along with a phone, computer, and printer."

"You've thought of everything."

"Not everything." The heat coming from his gaze caused Crystal's breath to catch in her throat.

As if he knew how he was affecting her, the heat turned to amusement. "Soon," he whispered. Regret tinged his voice. "First, I need to get you up to speed on this case."

She sat back in her chair. "So a sub's family is suing the Dominant, thinking there is abuse going on?"

"Yes. Sage is my client and the one being sued. Brady is her sub."

"Wait a second. Female Dom."

"Sage prefers Domme, pronounced dom-eh and spelled d-o-m-m-e with a capital D."

"What about Dominatrix?"

"A Dominatrix is a paid female Dominant." Jordan rested his chin on his fingers.

"Got it." Crystal made a mental note. This was going to be very interesting.

"Brady's family believes Sage is abusing him."

"If he's denied it, why is this going forward?" she asked.

"That's why it's civil and not criminal. His family has decided it's a form of domestic violence and abuse. They've made a case, and because there's no standing law in the state, it's been allowed to go forward."

"And Washington State doesn't have a Strategic Lawsuit Against Public Participation or SLAPP law. You mentioned depositions are next week?"

"Yes. We've completed initial interrogatories and discovery. The prelim in two weeks will determine if the case will move forward."

Crystal pulled out her phone and opened her note application. "I'm jotting down some notes on what I'll need to research." She didn't know much about Dominant/submissive relationships outside of the books she'd read, but she'd get up to speed.

"I have a list of kink-friendly professionals you can contact, especially other lawyers. I've reached out to a few; none have had any experience with this type of civil case."

"You're a kink-friendly professional." She hadn't heard the term before, but it made sense, especially since kink and abuse were often confused.

"I am."

Was he also part of the kink community? He didn't say, but Crystal thought he might be. He was friends with Max, after all. So what did that mean? She was friends with Sierra and wasn't into kink except for reading about it. And she had asked Sierra if she could get her inside Max's club, because she was curious. Was Jordan a member?

"Sorry, I missed what you said?" Her cheeks turned warm. She was so lost in her head she hadn't been paying attention.

"I said this is a delicate case, and I'd like to protect the kink community and avoid perpetuating stereotypes as much as possible."

"I understand. What people do in their private lives should be exactly that—private."

"Exactly. Misconceptions run rampant when it comes to the kink community. Some people think its abuse or worse."

Crystal tilted her head. "Sierra told me everything is consensual, and if it is, then why object to it? People should enjoy what they enjoy."

"Even if they're into pain?"

She frowned. "I guess. I don't see the point in causing someone pain."

"I can see you'll need some education." A knock sounded at the door. Valerie stuck her head in. "Mr. Frost, your eleven o'clock appointment is here."

Crystal glanced at the time on her phone. She'd been here almost two hours.

"Thank you, Valerie. I'll be out in a moment." The door closed. "I hate to cut this short."

"I understand." Crystal slipped her phone back in her bag and zipped it shut. Jordan was at her side when she stood. Awareness shot through her body. "Kendra will be here when you get here tomorrow. She'll show you the office and get you all set up. You'll have access to the case files. I should be in around one, unless my court case takes longer."

"Perfect." Maybe by then she would have her unruly body under control.

"And Crystal?" He tugged her to a stop at the door.

She looked up at him.

"Professional in the office, but outside of it, I make no guarantees."

"You're assuming a lot, Jordan."

"Am I?"

"Yes." She took a deep breath. "I'm my own woman. You should realize that by now. So don't make assumptions." She swept by him and out of the room. Kendra was waiting by the reception desk with her raincoat and a manila envelope. "Thank you," Crystal said, taking the items from Kendra.

It wasn't until Crystal got to her car that she realized her nerves were still tingling from her encounter with Jordan.

Resisting him was not going to be easy. This was not good. Not at all.

Chapter Two

Jordan Frost was glad when his client left. He'd barely been able to keep up with the conversation. His mind was on the curvy, sexy Crystal Hayden. He'd been surprised when she answered the ad for a paralegal.

He was glad she did. Working with her would be an experience. She came highly recommended. He'd glanced at her resume, but the recommendations looked stellar. The night they had talked over coffee, he'd enjoyed her humor and her spice. A woman who wasn't afraid to take a stand.

He'd intervened when she confronted the arguing couple, but it was more to protect her than anything else. He had no idea if the father was abusive. Jordan shook his head. His sexism was showing. The mother could be abusive as well.

Crystal had voiced her displeasure at his intervention, even as he walked her to her ride. She was passionate. He wanted to channel her passion into his bed. A grin took over his lips.

The interview hadn't been conventional. Normally, he would have let Kendra handle it, but the job he needed Crystal to do was a little unconventional as well. He needed someone he could trust and who could work without constant direction. Crystal fit the bill. And if he was able to coax her into his bed, why not?

Her job was safe. He wanted her to be comfortable with the knowledge. So adding the clause about her job being safe to the employment contract didn't bother him at all. He wouldn't harass her on the job, but after hours... He'd entice her to play with him.

Scallywag. Jordan heard his mother's voice in his head. That's what she'd called him when he got into trouble as a child. He shook his head. His mother would have liked Crystal.

Jordan missed his mother.

A frown marred his forehead. He still had to return the phone call from the Washington State corrections office. He was sure it was about his father, and Jordan didn't care if the man rotted in jail for murdering his mother.

Leaning back in his chair, Jordan didn't even notice the mountains gleaming with snow. There had been no signs of what set his father off that fateful day. Oh, his father had a temper, would yell at him and his mother, but he'd never raised a hand to either of them. Until that day. Seeing his mother's broken body on the floor caused Jordan to descend into a cold silence. He'd called the police and watched them cart his father away. Thanks to some neighbors, they helped him get his mother taken care of. He didn't even tell his father about the funeral. Jordan had no contact of any kind with his father and hadn't seen him since the day he was sentenced. And that was how Jordan wanted it.

He exhaled and shook his head to clear his thoughts. He picked up Crystal's resume and read it to get his mind back where it belonged. Oh, yes, she had impressive credentials. He frowned when he saw the last law firm she'd worked for. Why had she left? The Stevenson Group was one of the best-known law firms in Seattle, and they paid top dollar.

Jordan made a note on the ever-present notepad on his desk and kept reading. Her schooling was excellent, as were her references. He frowned. High school was in Kansas. Interesting. She wasn't a native Washingtonian.

Well, one thing for sure, life was going to be a lot more exciting with her around.

* * * *

"So how did the job interview go?" Sierra asked over dinner. Since she and her boyfriend, Max, were at the club on Friday and Saturday nights, Sierra, Tessa, and Crystal had moved girls' night from Friday to Monday so they could all have dinner.

Crystal hesitated. What would her friends think? She took a deep breath. "It was with Jordan's law firm."

"What?" Tessa's eyes went wide.

"Did it not go well? You two sort of had a fight the night we had coffee together," Sierra said.

"Actually, it went really well." Out of this world, if she was honest. The man caused her smoldering libido to roar into a blazing fire. One she was trying to keep under control.

"Did you take the job?" Tessa asked.

"I did." Crystal looked at her friends.

"But…" Tessa prompted.

"That's great." Sierra held up her wine glass. "To Crystal's new adventure." Glasses clinked, and they drank.

"You were pretty mad at him that night," Tessa said.

"Water under the bridge." At least it was now. Had she known the interview was with Jordan, she might have canceled. Maybe it was a good thing she hadn't

21

known. This new job intrigued her, and so did the man she was working with.

"What kind of case will you be helping Jordan with?" Sierra asked.

"I can't discuss the case." Crystal shook her head. NDA or not, she never discussed an ongoing case with anyone, not until it was settled and then only the barest public details.

"I don't see how you'll be able to work with him all day after what happened when we had coffee together," Tessa said.

"I don't think Jordan is a bad guy." She reached over and patted Tessa's hand. "You worry too much, my friend." Maybe Tessa was right to be worried, especially if one considered how she'd reacted to Jordan. He was damn sexy. "He thought he was doing the right thing." Crystal could see it now; at the time, however, her emotions were too involved.

Tessa huffed and sat back in her seat. Sierra smiled, and Crystal fought not to blush or squirm in her seat at the gleam in Sierra's eyes.

"Now that we've quizzed Crystal, have you both finished reading our book club selection yet?" Sierra asked.

"Yes." Tessa laughed. "I can't wait for the next meeting. This is so fun."

Crystal relaxed in her seat. At least Jordan was no longer a topic of discussion.

* * * *

Crystal walked into the law offices at seven forty-five. Valerie was at her desk, and Kendra was there talking to her.

"Good morning," Crystal said, setting the box of

goodies on Valerie's desk. "I brought donuts and scones for the office." She smiled at the two women. "I would have brought coffee, but I'm not sure what everyone drinks. Jordan mentioned he would be in court this morning."

"Yes, and thank you so much. I was running late this morning and couldn't stop for food," Valerie said.

"That was very nice of you," Kendra said.

"I hope I got enough." Crystal had revisited the firm's website last night, and while the lawyers were listed, she made an educated guess at how much support staff there was.

"I'm sure you did." Kendra opened up the box and nodded to Valerie, who used a napkin and picked out a scone. "Let me show you to your office and then give you the tour. First stop after your office will be the break room. Everyone is going to love you for these treats."

Crystal picked up her bag and coffee and followed Kendra down the hallway. Kendra balanced the box and pushed open an office door. Crystal stopped in the doorway. So not what she was expecting.

This was a lawyer's office, not a paralegal's. She was used to workspaces like Valerie's, out in the open and where anyone could see her. A big oak desk sat in front of a bigger window and a new leather chair. A laptop was already on the desk, with a monitor attached.

There was a small side table and below it was a small refrigerator. The other wall had two file cabinets and an empty bookcase.

"Is everything okay?" Kendra asked, looking back at Crystal.

"Oh yes." Crystal crossed the room and set everything on the gleaming wood. "I wasn't expecting something this big or private."

"It is nice." Kendra smiled and held out the keyring. "This is the key to your office; the other key unlocks the main office door. The small gold one is for your desk, and the silver one for the file cabinets."

"Thank you."

"I left your passwords to get into the computer and onto the company network in the top desk drawer. The laptop is already paired to the monitor and the printer. If you have any problems, let me know."

"Thank you. Makes things easy for me." Crystal stepped into the office and put her bag under the desk, before returning to Kendra.

"All right. Office layout." Kendra stepped out the door. "Jordan's office is right here." She pointed to the closed door at the next office. Then they started walking. By the time they made it to the break room, Crystal had been introduced to most of the staff.

Kendra walked Crystal back to her office. "If you need anything, find me or ask Valerie."

"I will. Thank you." Okay, she'd get settled and see what she needed. Rounding the desk, she sat down and sighed. Luxury. This was a chair made for an executive.

She opened the top drawer. The passwords were right where Kendra said, but there was also a big envelope with her name on it.

Crystal pulled both out and opened the envelope first to find a file folder and a letter inside.

> *Crystal,*
> *Sorry I'm not there*
> *for your first morning in*
> *the office. I trust that*

Kendra has shown you around. The file folder has some information related to the case to get you started on your research. If you need anything, ask Kendra or Valerie.

See you later today.

J.

As she read the letter, she heard Jordan's husky voice, and her body reacted. Goosebumps rose over her skin. *Get it together.*

Crystal set the letter aside, booted up the laptop, and signed in. She took a sip of her coffee and a bite of her scone as she read the documents in the folder. A frown appeared. What was he talking about? There were a lot of acronyms. She'd have to research them to even get started.

First things first. She opened her company email box to make sure everything there looked good. She'd had trouble in enough temp jobs so she made sure she could access email and the company server. Everything worked like a charm.

Opening the internet, she typed in the first acronym, RACK, and hit enter. Several things came up. And not one of them made sense. She frowned. Okay, this was going to be fun trying to figure this all out. She opened the side drawer of the desk, empty. She tried the next one. It, too, was empty.

All right, first thing on her to-do list was office supplies. Crystal drained her coffee and left her office. Kendra's door was closed so she went to see Valerie, who was on the phone, nodding and writing. When she hung up she looked at Crystal. "Is there a problem?"

"Office supplies?"

"Oh, sorry, I didn't think of that." She started to stand, but the phone rang again. Crystal watched her take care of the call. Busy firm. Good to know. When Valerie hung up, Crystal said, "Point me in the right direction."

"File room, there's another small room attached where we keep the supplies."

"Got it." Crystal went down the hallway. She found the supply room easily. Thankfully there was a cart in the room. She got what she needed and took it back to her office.

When she came up for air, it was almost eleven. Crystal stood and stretched. She'd go ask Valerie if there was a good place nearby to grab a sandwich or something. Gathering her wallet, she walked out to Valerie. A man was standing in front of Valerie's desk, his face slightly red, and Valerie looked uncomfortable.

"I don't care for excuses. If you continue to mess things up, I'll fire you."

One of the other lawyers, Crystal surmised, but still, why was he yelling at Valerie?

"Excuse me," Crystal said. "What is the issue?" Crystal raised her chin when the man turned his glacial gaze on her.

"Who are you?" he demanded.

"Crystal Hayden, Mr. Frost's paralegal." She held out her hand, which was ignored. "And you are?" She kept her tone civil and even. It was hard, but she did it.

"Charles Johnson, I'm one of the partners in this firm, and I certainly didn't authorize a paralegal." His voice was loud and annoying.

Crystal stared at the man. Partner? As far as she

knew Jordan was the sole owner. "I work for Mr. Frost and no one else, but you didn't answer my question regarding the issue of why you're yelling at Valerie."

"I'd like to know as well," Kendra said walking up to the group.

"She's incompetent."

Crystal's hackles went up as Valerie cringed. "We've talked about this, Mr. Johnson," Kendra said, her voice soft but with a thread of hardness through it. "If you have an issue with personnel, you come to me."

"So you can ignore me," he spit out.

Crystal's BS radar hit max at his comment. She opened her mouth, but Kendra beat her to the punch.

"Excuse me, Mr. Johnson, but you're being deliberately rude. I believe you owe everyone an apology." Kendra put her hands on her hips.

He glared at them and pointed to Crystal. "Keep your nose out of something that isn't your business." Then he pointed between Valerie and Kendra. "And I'll be sure to talk to Jordan about you two." He turned and marched down the hallway.

"Go ahead," Kendra snapped after him. A minute later, an office door slammed shut.

Crystal sighed and looked at Valerie. "Are you okay?"

"Yeah. A little shaken up is all."

"Sorry you had to experience Johnson on your first day," Kendra said to Crystal.

"You can't help he's an ass. I've worked with his type before."

Kendra smiled. "Valerie, why don't you take a break and have the service handle any calls for right now."

"Okay." Valerie pressed several buttons on the phone. "I think I'll walk down to Carson's. Can I get you anything?"

"I'm good," Kendra said.

"Carson's?"

"Small coffee shop," Valerie said.

"May I walk with you? I was coming to ask you if there was someplace around here," Crystal said. She was glad Kendra was giving Valerie a break. Showed she was a good and compassionate office manager.

"Sure." Valerie grabbed her purse.

Kendra waved them off as they walked to the elevator.

"So where did you work before here?" Crystal asked as they walked down the street. One would never know yesterday had been cold and blustery. Today the sun was out, and while there was a chill in the air, it wasn't freezing. "Receptionist at the gym."

"Totally different worlds." Crystal knew how hard it could be. She'd been so out of her depth with her first job. Luckily she had a boss who took pity on her and put her into a better position. "How long have you been at the firm?"

"A little over a year." They reached a small coffee shop and walked in. By the time they got back to the office, they were chatting like old friends.

When they made their way to the reception desk, they noticed a tall, blond man standing there. "Oh please, don't tell me Johnson ran off another receptionist?"

"Ummm, no." Crystal said. "I'm Crystal Hayden, Mr. Frost's paralegal." She held out her hand.

"Martin Anderson." He took her hand.

"Mr. Anderson." Crystal smiled. Now this man

was cordial.

"Martin, please."

"Martin."

Valerie took her seat behind reception. "Don't let Johnson get to you," he said to Valerie.

Crystal blinked. "How did you know?"

"He's a pain. Even though you don't work for him, he'll do his best to trip you up." With that, he turned and walked down the hallway.

Interesting dynamic. Johnson was a jerk; Anderson seemed nice. And Jordan was… Crystal shook her head. No, she wouldn't think of Jordan as a potential romantic interest. "Lunch at one?" Crystal asked.

"Yes, sounds good," Valerie replied, and Crystal left the reception desk.

Crystal sat down at her desk and went back to researching acronyms. She wrote down the ones that didn't seem to make any sense to her.

When she started researching Dominants, lots of information came up, and she had no clue what link to click on. Next, she tried BDSM. Her eyes went wide. She went to different websites to read and ended up more confused. Oh, brother. This was going to be a steep learning curve. Determined to learn about the lifestyle, she wrote notes and kept going.

* * * *

Jordan let out a breath as he left the courthouse. Today had been a hell of a day in court. The case should have been routine, but it had dragged on for weeks because of a reluctant witness and a defendant who had decided at the last minute they wanted a full jury trial. The case was now with the jury, and he anticipated they would have a verdict in a day or so.

He took a cab back to his office. He'd hoped to be at the office at least part of the day to help Crystal, and as he made his way up to his office, he wondered how she'd faired. Crystal hadn't been very far from his thoughts today, and he was impatient to see her.

"Hi, Valerie," he said, as he walked into the reception area.

"Mr.—Jordan." She smiled. "Here are your messages." She held a stack out to him.

"Thank you. Everything go well today?"

"Yes."

"Not really."

Jordan turned to see Crystal standing in her office door. Damn, she was a sight for sore eyes.

"Oh?" He frowned, but Crystal shook her head. "Did you get settled in?"

"I did. I know you're just in from court, but if you have a minute?"

He nodded, then looked at Valerie. "Send the phone over to the service and go home. It's almost four-thirty, and I suspect you've had a busy day."

"Thank you." Valerie grinned. "Crystal, I'll grab coffee and snacks in the morning."

"Okay. Remember what I said."

"I will." Valerie hit a button on the phone, gathered up her things, and left.

"Why do I think your first day wasn't an easy one?" He pushed open his office door.

"It wasn't bad. Busy, but not bad." She followed him into his office.

He caught a whiff of her perfume, something with vanilla in it. It reminded him of baking cookies with his mother when he was little. "I take it something happened today." He dropped his briefcase on his desk and turned to look at Crystal.

"I'm not sure, but I'm assuming, because your name is the only one that appears on the firm header, you are the sole owner?

"I am." He rubbed the back of his neck, and his stomach rumbled. "I haven't had lunch, and I'm starving. Would you be willing to discuss all of this over dinner?"

She stared at him with concern in her gaze. "This can wait until tomorrow."

"I'm hungry, and you have to eat dinner. I suspect you have questions from some of your research today as well as about whatever happened in the office." He kept his gaze on her.

"I do."

"Then go get your things, and let's go eat." This was a good idea. They could discuss her concerns in private, and he could relax a bit.

"Oh, all right." She sighed and left his office. They met back up in reception. Crystal had her phone in her hand. "Where do you want me to meet you?"

Jordan thought for a moment before he rattled off an address. "Or you could follow me?"

"That works." They walked out. "Don't you have to lock up?"

"Anderson or Johnson will since they're usually the last ones out." The elevator pinged, and they got on. Once in the parking lot, Jordan pointed to his dark blue SUV. "That's me. What do you drive?"

"The small, green SUV over there." She was parked at the end of the lot.

"Okay, follow me. It won't take us long." He watched her move to her vehicle and get in before he got into his own. He'd have to make sure she got a spot closer to his. He didn't like that she parked in the back of the lot where there wasn't a lot of light. It was January and dark by four-thirty.

He started his SUV and backed out. When he glanced in his rear view mirror, she was right behind him. On the way home, he called in a pizza order to be delivered.

He kept glancing in his rear view mirror to make sure Crystal was still behind him. She was. When they stopped at a red light, he could see her frowning. The area they were in was residential with no restaurants. He hadn't said anything about eating at his house, probably because he didn't want her to refuse.

But damn, the argument could be made he'd lied by omission. If she wanted to go to a restaurant, they'd go. He wanted to know what happened in the office from her perspective—because he was sure he had an email from Kendra about it—and what questions she had. Both conversations were best done in private. He made a left and then a right before turning into his driveway.

He began to relax as his small home came into view, and a sense of peace invaded him. He'd been lucky to score this house. He didn't like apartment living, and it was close enough he didn't have a long drive to the club.

Jordan parked, got out, and waited for Crystal to park. "Where are we?" she asked as she stepped out of her car, slinging her bag over her shoulder.

"My house."

"Jordan."

He held up his hand. "I should have said something before we left the office. I'm sorry. I blame my tired and hungry brain. Also, we need privacy if we're going to talk about the case."

She nodded. "We could have gone into one of the conference rooms and ordered food to be delivered."

"Agreed, we could have." He sighed. "My mistake. If you want, we can go back to the office." His shoulders slumped a bit.

"Okay, you're off the hook. But this is a one-time pass."

He smiled. "Thank you. I ordered pizza. It should be here in fifteen minutes." He cupped her elbow and walked to the front door.

"Sure of me, were you?"

"Hopeful, besides I could always eat the pizza tomorrow."

Inside, he shut off the alarm.

"Come on." He guided her into the family room. "Make yourself comfortable. If you don't mind, I want to go change out of my court clothes."

"All right." Her voice was soft as she looked around the room. Jordan turned and jogged to his bedroom, hoping she wouldn't run for the door while he was gone.

* * * *

Crystal hadn't expected this at all. When Jordan said dinner, she pictured someplace in town, not his home. Her stomach twisted itself around. She was alone with him.

Needing a distraction, she wandered around. His home was another surprise. She'd figured he had one of those new loft apartments, but no. Instead, they were in an older residential area of Pleasant Valley, an area she'd been scoping out for a house of her own.

Jordan's home was one of the old-fashioned log

cabin types. The family room had a vaulted ceiling with beautiful exposed beams. There was a light brown leather sofa and love seat, and what looked like a very well broken in recliner.

A large TV was mounted on the wall. Crystal turned around slowly. Tall windows let in natural light, except it was dark now, but she'd bet, during summer, the room was awash with light.

She spied the entrance to the kitchen and the hallway Jordan had gone down to go change. Setting her bag next to the sofa, Crystal slipped off her shoes and sank onto the cushions.

The butter soft leather cupped her body. Ah, this was heaven. She hadn't realized how tired she was. It had been a while since she'd put in a full day at an office. With a sigh, she leaned her head back and stared at the ceiling. She should be mad Jordan didn't tell her they were going to his home for dinner. He was right. They needed total privacy for this discussion. She wished he'd told her before they left the office.

She jumped when she heard footsteps. Sitting up straight, she brushed her hands down her shirt.

"I'm a bad host. What would you like to drink?" He strode through the family room to the kitchen and flipped on the light.

Crystal's mouth dried out. Jordan in a suit was one thing, but in sweats and a Washington State t-shirt, her mind went right into the gutter. The t-shirt molded to his chest and showed off his toned arms. His sweats, while a little loose, didn't hide his fine ass. He looked deliciously lickable.

"I have beer, wine, soda, and water," he called out from the kitchen. "What's your poison?"

It took her a minute to realize he was talking about something to drink. "Beer please." She should have water or soda, but she enjoyed beer with pizza. Plus, she was eating and wouldn't be driving for a while.

"Here you go." He handed her a tall glass filled with amber liquid.

"Thank you."

"You're welcome." He took a seat next to her. "You mentioned something happened at the office today? I haven't had a chance to read all my email yet."

"Yeah." She took a sip of her beer before setting it on the coaster on the side table. "Since you said you're the sole owner, I'm going with Johnson works for you."

"Yes. He came in about three years ago. I've been considering opening up to a partnership. What did he do?" Jordan set his beer down and looked at her. Tension in the room ratcheted up.

"Not so much me. I can take care of myself. But he was rude to Valerie and Kendra."

"What did he say?" Jordan's voice grew low and cold.

Crystal shivered. "He told Valerie she was incompetent. He said Kendra was ignoring his complaints, and he was a partner." Her voice filled with anger.

"Hey." He held his hands up. "I'm on your side. I'll talk with Johnson. I told him if he ran off another receptionist, there'd be hell to pay." The tension lessened.

"Thank you. Valerie works hard, and Kendra does too. They don't need this kind of crap."

"Oh?"

Crystal shifted under his pointed gaze. "I know not everything runs smoothly in an office, but I don't think a lawyer should abuse their staff." Why did she feel the weight of his stare like a naughty child sent to the principal's office? Although she wouldn't mind if Jordan took her over his knee.

Whoa! Where did *that* thought come from?

"Thank you for being honest with me, and I agree with you." The doorbell pealed, and Jordan jumped up. "Dinner. Be right back."

The interruption couldn't have come at a better time. What in the hell had she been thinking, envisioning Jordan spanking her? She worked for him, and even with a signed employment contract that said she had a job no matter what happened between them, they were still co-workers. Hadn't she learned workplace romances never worked?

The smell of pizza hit her senses before Jordan walked back into the room. Her stomach growled.

"Food. I wasn't sure what you liked, so I got half meat lovers and half cheese. Plus a salad." He slid the box onto the large wood coffee table. "I'll go grab some plates and utensils."

Crystal opened the salad box so it was ready when he came back. She dished up some salad, drizzled dressing over it, and took a slice of pizza. They ate in silence, both hungry. Jordan sat back after he finished off his fifth slice of pizza.

"I can't believe you ate five pieces," she said, closing the salad box.

"Breakfast was a muffin, and since I missed lunch, I was starving."

"What happened? You said you didn't plan to be in court all day."

"Problem with a witness." He turned toward her.

"Tell me about your research and what questions you have."

Crystal turned and adjusted her legs under her, making sure her skirt covered her legs. "Well, I started working with the acronyms you left me."

"Did they not make sense?"

"Hardly. I tried looking them up on the internet and became more confused."

"I see." He rubbed his chin.

Crystal's stomach churned. She wanted to work with Jordan, but if he was having second thoughts… "I'm sorry I'm not more informed about the lifestyle."

"Don't be. You were upfront with me. I'm trying to think of a way to bring you up to speed a bit quicker."

"I know what SSC and RACK mean—safe, sane, and consensual, and risk-aware consensual kink—but what does it mean in the lifestyle? Safe for whom? Sane? That can mean a million things. Consensual is self-explanatory. Isn't all of this a little subjective? Who decides what's safe or sane? I get the risk-aware part. You're aware of the risk but do it anyway as long as everyone consents."

"Where to start?" Jordan rubbed the back of his neck. "In the lifestyle, safe means safe for everyone—the Dominants and the submissives. SSC is a code within the community to protect everyone. Not everyone holds to it. In my opinion, the good ones do."

"Makes sense." It did now.

"Sane has to do with mindset. Is this a sane thing to do? For example: If a submissive asked me to use a cane on her back, would that be sane? Yes, but I'd be careful not to go near the kidneys and cause damage."

Crystal's gut tightened. "How dangerous is kink?"

She never thought about it.

"If you don't know what you're doing, it can be dangerous to everyone." Jordan leaned his elbows on his knees. "Training is important for both Dominants and submissives, along with a good place to play." He turned his head and looked at her. "Things like fire play, knife play, and rigging take time to learn and learn right."

"I have no idea what those are, but they sound dangerous." A shudder ran over her body.

"They can be, again, especially if someone doesn't know what they're doing." He rubbed his jaw. "I think I just thought of a way to help you understand faster." Jordan picked up his phone and began typing. "Should have an answer in a minute."

Crystal tilted her head, wondering who he'd texted, and then his phone pinged. He read the message and laughed.

"Here's the deal. What I'm about to tell you will be covered by another NDA, but not until Thursday. Can I trust you to keep quiet?"

"Of course. This has to do with the case so the NDA applies in my book. But what is Thursday?"

He nodded. "Thursday you are coming with me to a BDSM club."

Chapter Three

"What?" Crystal's heart sped up, and her nerves tingled with anticipation and apprehension. "Are you serious?"

"I am." He leaned forward. "You need to understand the lifestyle, and you can only get so much from reading."

"True. Are we going to Seattle?"

"No. I'm surprised Sierra hasn't told you."

Crystal lowered her eyes. "She did. But I don't want her to get into trouble. I know because I was making sure she was safe with Max."

Jordan smiled. His warm fingers ran over her cheek, causing her skin to tingle. "Look at me, Crystal." He waited until she was looking at him. "It's okay. The NDA Sierra signed covers talking about who is at the club doing what. We figured people would talk about the club itself. We wanted to protect the people at the club."

"We? Who is this we?"

"Max, Damon, and myself. We're more or less partners in the club." He shifted closer to her. "Since we're talking about this, are you interested in learning more about kink?"

"In relation to the case?" Had he moved even closer? Yes, he had. She was sitting with her legs tucked under her, and his knees were now almost touching hers.

"More than the case." His palm slid around to the back of her neck.

Her nerves danced with excitement and a hint of anxiety. Did she want to explore kink personally? To find out if kink was as good in real life as it was in the books she'd read or from what Sierra told her? To trust someone—she'd read the lifestyle was about trust—that much? Yes, to all of it. After reading about it and seeing how happy Sierra was, she wanted to know more. Still, in the back of her mind, she could hear her mother's words: *Sex is a sin.*

"You're thinking very hard," Jordan said.

"I am." He stroked the back of her neck. "Jordan, this is inappropriate." She wiggled beneath his touch.

"Why? I'm attracted to you."

"No." Crystal rose to her feet and tried to control her breathing. Her thoughts were starting to jumble together. The case, his offer, his touch, everything.

"Crystal." He frowned.

"If this has to do with the case, fine, but anything else is a no-go." *But I want it*, a little voice inside her said. Yes, part of her wanted to explore with Jordan, but she couldn't. They barely knew each other. However, it was more than that. Her upbringing hadn't been one of a loving nature. While she'd gotten past certain aspects of her teen years, Jordan brought out memories best left in the past.

Jordan stared at her. "All right." She released the breath she didn't realize she'd been holding. "For now. Tomorrow I'll have you sign the NDA for the club and fill out the paperwork for a background check."

"Background check?" She remembered Sierra talking about the NDA and other stuff, but she hadn't gone into detail. Crystal sat back down.

"Yes. It's a private club. You'll be my guest, but

you still have to fill out the background check and NDA, and even though you're not becoming a member, the club application, and go over the rules. We'll go over them tomorrow and go to the club on Thursday."

"You seem to have it all planned out."

"I do." He leaned in. "Tell me, Crystal, what scares you more: kink or my attraction to you?" His voice had dropped to a low, husky tone that sent shivers over her skin.

How the hell did she answer? It wasn't his attraction to her so much, but how she was reacting to him. Her willpower took a hike when she was around him, and it wasn't a good thing. "I'm scared of myself." The words slipped from her mouth before she could stop them.

His lips parted, and his breath whooshed out of him. "That was unexpected."

A tremor slid over her skin at his intense stare.

"You're breathing is a little shallow. Not sure if it's from excitement or fear, but I'm not going to lie to you. I'm a Dominant. And I'd like nothing more than to play with you." He leaned toward her.

And she wanted to play with him. She wanted to deny it, but she couldn't, not if she was honest with him and herself. Sinful. The word echoed in her mind.

Crystal froze. "Jordan." She placed her hands on his shoulders and pushed. "This is going way too fast." His words made her heart pound and her mouth go dry. Yes, it was too soon.

He moved back. "Is it?" He stared at her with those brown eyes of his. "Be honest with me. How am I making you feel right now?"

"Excited, scared, and a little bit out of control."

Words like *sinful and slut* ran through her head like a broken record. Would she ever get past those memories? Maybe it was time to see a therapist again? She'd have to think about it.

"Good emotions, all of them. What is scaring you?"

"Everything," she whispered. This was crazy. "Please scoot back." She needed some distance between them to regain her balance. Emotionally and physically.

"Why?"

"Because I can't breathe with you so close." It was true; she was having trouble getting a full breath. No man had ever affected her like he did. Even the first night they met, he'd done this to her.

"Thank you for being honest." He shifted until he was at the other end of the sofa.

Crystal blew out a breath. That was better. He wasn't so close she would be tempted. She froze. Tempted? Yep, she was tempted to jump into his arms. Oh, this was so not good. He was a lawyer. She'd promised herself never to date another lawyer after the last disaster. But still, how would she be able to look him in the eye? And there were her family hang-ups.

"Maybe this isn't such a good idea." She shifted and unfolded her legs. Her father's voice sounded in her head. *Time for the sin closet, you slut.*

"What's got you running?" His voice held concern.

"We shouldn't be doing this." She got to her feet and glanced at the beer sitting on the side table. She had barely finished half of it, so she couldn't blame being tipsy for what had happened here. "I should be going. Thank you for dinner. We can talk tomorrow."

"Very well." His voice was soft. Jordan stood and waited while she slipped on her shoes, then escorted her to the front door without touching her.

"I can make it to my car," she said as he stepped out with her.

"I'll walk you." He shut the door behind him. "I'm not sure why you're running, but I won't push you." Crystal wasn't going to say another word. This whole thing had made her uncomfortable. All she could remember was her father's anger at her. Tears gathered behind her eyes. She did this. She made Jordan angry with her.

Thank goodness she had her own vehicle. It would make it easier to escape. Yeah, she admitted to herself, she was escaping. At her vehicle, she unlocked it and tossed her bag and jacket onto the passenger seat before she turned to Jordan.

He was right there. In her space. Her hands came up, palms flat on his chest. Damn, she could feel his muscles through the shirt. "Jordan."

"I said I won't push tonight. We have time."

She wanted to ask him: Time for what? But he leaned down and brushed his lips over hers. It was a soft kiss, a barely there kiss, before he lifted his head. Her lips tingled, and her body shifted ever so slightly toward him.

"Drive carefully, and call me when you get home." He stepped away from her, and her hands fell to her sides.

Crystal climbed into her SUV, and Jordan shut the door. She started her vehicle, backed out of the space, and watched him in her rearview mirror until she couldn't see him.

His soft kiss carried a promise of more. Crystal

trembled. This was so not good. All the way home, she argued with herself over the kiss she wanted more of.

She got to her apartment and flopped down on the sofa, still unsure. What was she going to do tomorrow?

Act like nothing happened, that's what. She was a professional. She could do this.

She fished her cell out of her purse. He'd told her to call him. Wait a second; she didn't have Jordan's number. Well, she couldn't call him. Maybe she should call Sierra and ask for it. She didn't want him to worry. She started to scroll through her contacts and stopped.

When had he programmed his number into her phone? Because there it sat. Jordan Frost. She punched the button.

"Are you home?"

"Yes. When did you program your number into my phone?" Her voice was firm.

His husky laugh sent waves of awareness through her nerves. "I'm going to plead the Fifth. Sleep well, my Crystal. See you tomorrow."

The line went dead, and with it, Crystal's ire. How did he manage to do that all the time? She shook her head and then put her phone down. She had a lot to think about before tomorrow. The biggest issue was how far would she allow this attraction to Jordan to go, and could she get past her upbringing to explore kink with him?

* * * *

When he could no longer see the lights of Crystal's car, Jordan entered the house and moved down the hall to his home gym. He needed to work off some frustration. He wrapped his hands and pulled on his boxing gloves. Stepping up to the punching bag, he let go with a series of punches. Not hard, but not soft.

Once he was warmed up, he began to hit the bag harder and faster. Damn it! He'd moved too fast with Crystal. He should know better. She was apprehensive enough when he sprang bringing her to his home for dinner. That should have been enough to make him back off.

But no, he had to keep pushing. Yes, he was a Dominant, and pushing was a part of his makeup, but Crystal wasn't his. At least not yet. There was that arrogance once again. He had to find a way to balance his attraction to her and his need to move too fast.

He wasn't sure why he was so determined to pursue Crystal. He wasn't into commitment with his play partners. A normal Top/bottom relationship with no ties was fine with him. Crystal was different. He punched the bag. From the first time he met her, it seemed as though a string connected them. Made him want more than a Top/bottom relationship. He wanted more with her. Lots more.

Slow and steady. His hands followed his brain. Tomorrow, they'd go over the club's NDA and background check. Thursday, he'd introduce her to the club. His cock stirred. This had more to do with the case than him, he reminded himself.

They were going to have some long nights and weekend work sessions over the next couple of weeks. He wanted her to be comfortable with him, not jumping every time he made a move.

He needed to give her time to get used to being around him and for her to realize he wasn't going to take advantage of her. So no more surprises. If he wanted them to work at his place, then he'd ask her. He would make this work.

Of course he would. He wanted Crystal, but she had to consent to him. He wasn't going to take this any further without that because he wasn't an ass. He could control his baser urges.

He'd apologize to her tomorrow and keep things professional between them until she signaled differently.

* * * *

"Sierra, I need your help," Crystal said as she drove into work the next morning. She'd wrestled with herself all night. Thank goodness for Bluetooth headsets.

"What's up?" Sierra asked.

"It's about Jordan."

"What?"

Even though Crystal couldn't see Sierra, she heard the sharp intake of breath and the rustle of bedding. "Did I wake you?"

"No. Just a second." There were muffled sounds in the background and the closing of a door. "Okay, I'm in the bathroom. What has Jordan done?"

"Hell, I caught you with Max." She should have known.

Sierra laughed. "It's okay. I needed to get up anyway. Now spill."

Crystal pulled into the parking lot of Sweet and Savory, Lara's cafe. At least she could sit here and talk. "Well, I can't really talk about the case we're working on together, but I can tell you it involves kink, and Jordan wants to take me to the club tomorrow night."

Sierra squealed, and Crystal winced. "That's fantastic." There was a pause. "I'm fine, Max." Crystal smiled. She must have woken Max with her yell.

"Has something changed since you asked me if I would talk to Max about letting you see the club?"

"No, but this is different." Crystal stared out the windshield at the cafe. "I want to see what the club is like, but this is…Jordan."

"Are you saying Jordan wants to scene with you?"

Crystal took a deep breath. "I don't know. We talked—a little—about Dominants and subs."

Sierra squealed. "Welcome to my world."

"You better calm down or Max will break through the bathroom door to make sure you're okay."

"I'm fine, sweetie," Sierra yelled. "Look, I can't do this over the phone."

"Well, I have no choice. I have to be at work in twenty minutes, and Jordan wants to talk about what it means to go to the club tomorrow night. He talked about going over another NDA and background check before I can go to the club."

"Okay. The NDA is easy, as is the background check. You'll pass with flying colors." Sierra's long breath floated over the airwaves. "Listen, be honest with him. Don't freak out. You'll see. It's close to the books we read, only more in-depth. Every little detail spelled out."

"Why doesn't that make me feel better?" Maybe she should tell Jordan to forget it. She could do the job without knowing kink. "You know how I was brought up." While their childhoods had been different, they shared a past filled with dysfunctional family life.

"It will be fine. Listen to Jordan and follow your instincts." Sierra lowered her voice. "Ignore the negative voices in your head. I never thought I'd find myself in the lifestyle, but Max convinced me to try, and I'm not sorry I did."

Crystal rubbed her stomach when it grumbled.

"Yeah, and I know you're happy."

"Deliriously."

"Thanks, Sierra. I'll let you get back to whatever you and Max were doing."

Sierra laughed. "Girls' dinner tonight. I want to hear all about this." The line went dead, and Crystal got out of her vehicle. Coffee and food were the first order of business, but her mind kept focusing in on Sierra's words: *Follow your instincts.*

After getting coffee and food, Crystal made her way to the office. She stepped out of her SUV and walked around to the passenger side. Before she could open the door, someone walked up to her car. Her head jerked up. Jordan stood there in all his tall, handsome, overwhelming glory.

"Sorry, didn't mean to scare you."

"It's okay." Her heart pounded, and she wanted to believe it was from the fright he gave her not how damn sexy the man looked in slacks and a polo shirt. She reached in and grabbed her bag, slung it over her shoulder, then reached back in for the coffee tray and box of food.

"Let me help." Jordan took the coffee tray from her and stepped back.

Crystal smiled. "Thank you." She shut the door and locked her vehicle.

"It was nice of you to stop for treats." He eyed the box and the tray of coffee cups. "You do know there is a pot in the break room," he said as they walked side-by-side into the building.

"I do." The elevator opened, and they stepped in. "But I love the way Lara makes a cafe mocha, and who can resist her carrot cake muffins?"

Jordan's laugh was rich and deep, sending shivers of awareness over her skin. "There are three cups here."

"Yep. One for me, a latte for Valerie, and an espresso for you." The elevator arrived at their floor, and she stepped out with Jordan following.

"Good morning," Valerie said when they entered the reception area.

"Morning." Crystal turned and pulled one of the cups out of the holder. "Your latte and muffin." She handed both to Valerie.

"Thank you so much. I was running late again today, so I forgot to stop." Valerie looked at Jordan. "I've cleared your schedule for this morning."

"Thank you, Valerie." Jordan looked at Crystal. "Shall we get started?"

Damn. He wasn't even going to give her a chance to gather her scattered thoughts. "I guess. Let me put the food in the break room, leave my bag in my office, and grab a note pad."

"Of course. Conference room one." He opened the box and stole a muffin, then took the coffee tray from her and sauntered away.

With a sigh, Crystal dropped off the food, grabbed her own muffin, and went to her office. She stowed her bag, then picked up a notebook and a pen.

She stopped inside the doorway of the conference room.

Jordan stood next to the small conference table, their coffee and three folders on the table in front of him.

"Why the conference room?" she asked.

"I want us to be comfortable as we talk." He gestured for her to take a seat, then shut the door behind her.

Crystal fought to keep her breathing slow and even. She sat down, turned to her left and placed her notebook and pen on the table. She picked up her coffee cup and took a long drink. The chocolate exploded on her tongue, and the espresso perked her up.

Jordan sat down facing her. "You're nervous."

"Good guess." She was. "I'm not sure about this, Jordan."

"I am." He sipped his coffee. "You need to understand the lifestyle so you can ask the right questions."

That much was true. "I get that. But the whole attraction thing, that's what I'm not sure about."

"I pushed last night, and I'm sorry." He sat his cup down. "I usually know when to back off."

"This is all so new. Different." Crystal tried to find the right words. *Trust your instincts.* Sierra's words came to mind.

"I know." He reached over and captured her left hand in his right. "I'll try to take things slower."

"That would be nice." She bit her lower lip. "Before we go any further with this, I want you to understand." She took a deep breath. Time to jump into the deep end. "I may be interested in the lifestyle and in being your sub. I need time to process it all." The words rushed out of her.

"Agreed." He squeezed her hand. "If I'm pushing you, say yellow."

"A safe word."

"Yep. I will instantly understand and adjust. Are you okay with that?"

Follow your instincts. "Yes."

"Good. For this morning, I want to go over the

NDA, background check, and application with you and get you all set up for Thursday night. Then go over the rules and questionnaire so you understand how this all relates to the case." He released her hand.

"I think I can handle it." A grin overtook his lips and made her insides turn over. She was glad she'd talked to Sierra about this.

"Then let's start." He picked up the first folder. "NDA, background check, club application."

* * * *

Jordan watched as Crystal read the NDA, then filled out the background check and application while she drank her coffee and munched on her muffin. He was happy she was being open and honest with him. Those new to the lifestyle sometimes had a problem with the degree and depth of honesty required. Pride coursed through him as well. Some things made Crystal obviously nervous, but she didn't let it hold her back. He liked that about her.

His dick twitched as Crystal bit her lower lip. Damn if that wasn't sexy to him. He couldn't wait until he could run his tongue over her mouth and soothe the sting of her bite. Hell, he wanted to use his tongue in other places too.

He reined his thoughts in. Hadn't he promised to go slow? He flexed his fingers around his coffee cup. She wasn't his sub…not yet.

She wasn't ready for his dominance. He needed to give her time to adjust before he went full Dom on her. Even so, suppressing his dominant side was difficult. Jordan polished off his own coffee and muffin. But he hungered for her, not food.

"Done." She handed the folder back to him.

"Thank you." He picked up the next folder. "Why don't you start reading this while I send the background check out." He handed her the new folder, stood, and left the room.

Jordan scanned the document and checked the file.

Yep, perfect. Closing it, he emailed it to Logan, a police officer, who did the background checks for the club. He walked back into the conference room. Crystal was bent over, reading. He waited for her to say something, but she didn't.

The flipping of pages sounded loud in the quiet room. Occasionally, she would pause, make a little check mark, and go on.

Jordan waited.

When she got to the end, she flipped the pages back to the beginning and tapped the end of the pen against her rosy lips. Her cheeks were a little pink.

Jordan waited.

She sighed and looked up. "This questionnaire is extensive. I'm going to need help understanding all of this."

Finally.

He wasn't sure she was going to ask questions or run screaming from the conference room. "Of course." He adjusted his chair so he was closer to her. "What do you need help with?"

"Everything." She stared at him, confusion in her green eyes. "I know this has to do with the case. But why so many questions?"

"In order for a Dom to understand what a sub is interested in, the questions are necessary."

"But don't you negotiate a scene together before

you do it?"

"A Dom and sub do negotiate, but there is also this list." He gestured toward the questionnaire. "This list is a little like a blueprint. In addition to limits, it gives the Dom an idea of what the sub enjoys and works as a sort of starting point when a Dom and sub are playing together for the first time."

"Isn't negotiation about that?"

"Yes, but think about it. A Dom and sub are going to play. Their negotiation could take hours to go over everything. This way, the Dom is already aware of the sub's hard limits, wants, and desires."

Crystal tilted her head. "Makes sense. Does the sub get to see the Dom's questionnaire?"

"If they ask, yes. I can't speak for everyone in the lifestyle. I do encourage the subs I train to ask to see the Dominant's questionnaire. You never want to play with someone you don't trust."

"Wait a second." Crystal shifted, turning more toward him. "If you play with someone you trust… Are you saying the Doms in your club don't hook up with subs?"

"Not in the traditional sense."

"Please explain, because now I'm even more confused."

"You've gotten most of your information from the books you read, and that's fine." He held up his hand when she started to talk. "When Max, Damon, and I started the club, we did so for a reason."

"Right. You mentioned Damon being involved last night."

"The three of us were tired of the hook-ups we saw at parties. We wanted the club to be a place where people could explore the lifestyle without pressure, but also with a sense of trust."

"The NDA, background checks, questionnaire, agreeing to the rules, it's all part of it?"

She caught on fast. "It is. The club itself is private. In order to become a member, you must know a member or someone in the kink community who knows us."

"That makes sense. You can vet people better."

"There are classes we require people to take. We don't have any new members coming in right now, or I'd have you sit through the classes that pertain to the club so you'd have a better understanding for the case. Max and I agreed I could explain to you as we go."

"What are the classes?"

"First one is what we are doing here, the NDA, background check, and limits list. The other classes are going over rules, expectations and then, finally, a night at the club."

"So how are we going to do it?" Her cheeks turned pink, and he hid a smile.

Jordan enjoyed explaining all of this to her. Her questions were intelligent. "Tomorrow night, I'll take you into the club as my guest. Usually it takes about a week to get the background check back, but I asked my contact to rush it."

"So I'll be able to see the club and what goes on. Am I allowed to talk to people?"

"Of course you are." He smiled. "You will be my guest, and it has not been conclusively established if you are a Dominant of submissive. Also, you are not in a committed D/s relationship, so lifestyle protocols don't apply to you." Jordan paused. "One thing to remember, however. If you wish to speak with a sub or slave, protocol and courtesy mandates you ask their Dom's or Master's permission."

Crystal wrinkled her nose "I think I have a lot to learn."

He wanted to gather her into his arms and kiss her, but they were in the office. "You don't have to learn everything today, but I would like to get through the questionnaire." He couldn't get distracted from what he was supposed to be doing. He shifted, trying to ease the pulsing of his cock.

"I'd like to take this"—she patted the folder that held the questionnaire and rules—"back into my office and review it more." There was a flash of hesitation in her eyes.

"Care to share why?"

"I would feel more comfortable. If I have any questions, I'll ask you."

Jordan looked at his watch. It was almost eleven. They'd been in the conference for three hours, and he should prep for his afternoon appointment. "All right. But we will need to discuss it before we leave tonight."

"I can do that." She sprang from her chair as if something had stung her. "Thanks." Crystal bolted from the room, leaving Jordan shaking his head. He quickly cleaned up and made his way back to his office. Time to get to work and not think about Crystal at the club and at his mercy.

A familiar tightening reminded him this would be no easy task.

* * * *

Crystal was never so glad to escape to her office. One more minute with Jordan and she would have kissed him silly. The man had no clue how sexy he was. She could barely think when he touched her, even in a non-sexual way.

Maybe it wasn't a bad thing, but not in the office. In the office, they needed to be professional. She laughed as she dropped to her chair and placed the folder on her desk. As if what they'd talked about was professional in the context of the case.

Her cell rang, and she fished it out of her bag. She wasn't surprised to see it was Sierra. "Hey there."

"I've been calling you for hours. Where have you been?"

"In the conference room with Jordan, discussing the club."

"Ohhh."

"Sierra, I'm doing this in a professional capacity. I need to understand what goes on."

"Right. Have you forgotten our conversation from this morning?"

"Of course I haven't, but…the questionnaire is intimidating." It was more than that. Her upbringing around sex made it difficult for her to think logically at times. Her parents' views on sex had been drummed into her. Sex was to only take place between a married couple. Crystal shivered. She had walked the straight and narrow while at home. Well, pretty much. But once she got out on her own, her eyes had been opened.

The few times she'd had sex in college, she'd approached it more as an experiment. With Jordan, it was different. He wasn't an experiment; he was dynamite. He could rock her world if she let him. *Slut*. The word slipped into her mind, and she pushed it away. There was no sin closet here and never would be.

"Yes, it is. Did you go through it?"

"Not completely. I convinced Jordan to let me take it to my office to finish up. I don't know how I didn't spontaneously combust at some of those questions." And there were those questions she had no clue what they meant.

Sierra laughed. "I have time right now. Do you want to go over it with me on the phone?"

Thank goodness for best friends. "Oh God, yes, that would be helpful." The less she had to ask Jordan, the better off for her own self-preservation. Crystal sat forward and opened the folder. "I understand hard limits, but some of these questions are way out of my scope. Like canes, crops, floggers, hairbrush, paddles…"

"All impact play. Let me explain."

"How do you know all of this?"

"Max has been teaching me, and after a couple times at the club, you'll begin to understand. So these are all things that can be used on you."

"Like hell." A chill raced up her spine as she remembered the times her father had hit her with his belt.

"It's not abuse. I kind of felt the same way, but think about the last book we read for the book club. Remember how the hero was flogging the heroine."

Crystal closed her eyes. Damn, the scene had made her squirm, in a good way. "Flogging maybe, but canes, crops, or other things? I don't think I can handle."

"I get it. You'll see all sorts of things at the club, so keep an open mind. What's next?"

For the next hour, Sierra went over the questionnaire with her. There were still some things they had to look up on the internet.

"Done." Crystal closed the folder. Damn, she

hadn't worked so hard over something in a while. She had notes on everything, so there was little she'd need to ask Jordan about. What a relief. The less time they spent discussing things like sex and kink, the better she'd be able to keep her attraction to him under wraps.

"Good. I'll be at the club tomorrow night."

"I thought you didn't go on Thursdays?"

"I usually don't, but I want to be there to support you."

"You are the best." It would make her less nervous if her best friend was there. "You and Max aren't going to play, are you?" She wasn't sure how she felt about seeing her friend and her friend's boyfriend in that situation.

"What are you going to wear?"

"I…oh shit. I can't wear what you wore. So not me." How could she have forgotten how Sierra was dressed that first night? Oh no. This wasn't going to work. She couldn't show off her body like that. But she wasn't going to the club to play. She was there to observe and learn for the case.

"Easy, Crystal. I'm sure we can find something in your closet. You have a little black dress, if I remember right."

"I do." She'd bought it for a song on sale a few years back. Crystal blew out a breath.

"It will work, and I'm sure Jordan will discuss it with you. You're going in the capacity of learning about kink for your case, nothing more."

Crystal wasn't sure she wanted to have this conversation. She was so out of her depth with Jordan. "Right, research to learn about it." Why did she have to keep reminding herself of that?

"Oh crap, Crystal, I have to go. I forgot I'm meeting a client. We still on for girls' night?"

"It's Wednesday. Book club night." Crystal remembered because she was looking at her calendar.

"That's right. Okay, see you at the book club." Sierra hung up.

Crystal set her phone on her desk. It was almost two. Maybe she'd take lunch and go check out the boutique down the street to see what they had for clothing. But first things first. She put aside the questionnaire and her notes from the call, then picked up the folder with the signed club rules and went into reception.

"Valerie, is Jordan with a client?"

"No, but he left for a meeting."

"Okay, I'm going to drop this folder on his desk and then go to lunch myself." She strode into Jordan's office, set the folder under his keyboard, then walked back out. "Did you go to lunch?" she asked Valerie.

"Not yet, but I will. I'm waiting for a client to arrive for Johnson's one-thirty appointment to show up before I go."

"All right, make sure you go. You need a break too." Crystal walked back into her office and grabbed her bag before leaving.

A brisk walk for three blocks and she found the little boutique. She stepped inside and looked around, hoping she could find something in here to wear.

"Hello, can I help you?" The voice belonged to a young woman with purple and pink hair who was coming out from the back of the store.

Crystal thought for a moment. "Maybe you can. I'm looking for something sexy and revealing, yet not too revealing."

The young woman tapped her chin with her finger. "I'm guessing something for a night out, going dancing and clubbing?"

"Sounds perfect." Just what she needed, someone who understood.

"Got it. Let's see what I have. If you'll follow me."

Forty minutes later, Crystal walked out of the boutique with a smile and a large bag. She wondered how Jordan would react when he saw her in the outfit she'd bought. Crystal shook her head; his reaction had nothing to do with it. It was an outfit for a later date so that when—and if—they played together, she'd fit in and not be the odd woman out like she'd been most of her life. Especially if she let Jordan into her life.

Her nerves danced in excitement. It was going to be a long wait until tomorrow night.

Chapter Four

Crystal paced around her apartment. Jordan had insisted on picking her up to go to the club. She'd put her coat on, not wanting Jordan to see what she was wearing until they reached the club. Hopefully he wouldn't think her black dress was too conservative.

He'd offered yesterday to send her an outfit, but she told him it was fine, she had one. He raised his eyebrows, but didn't say anything. Crystal smiled. Jordan was going to be surprised.

A knock sounded on her door. She checked to see who it was, then opened the door. "Hi, Jordan. I'm ready." She picked up her small purse.

"So I see." He stared at her. "Don't I get a preview?" His eyes gleamed with mischief.

"No." She shut the door behind her and locked it.

"You torture me, fair lady," he said, placing his hand over his heart.

"Dramatic much?" She couldn't suppress her laughter.

"I got you to laugh." He took her by the elbow and guided her to the elevator, then out to his SUV.

"What will happen when we get there?" She tangled her fingers in her lap.

"Nervous?" He covered her hands with one of his.

"A bit."

"Tonight is for you to see the club and what goes on. Remember, if you want to talk to a sub or slave, you will need to talk to their Dom or Master first."

"Okay." She'd spent all day reviewing the case, and getting a better understanding of the lifestyle would help the case. Her nerves tingled. This was about more than the case, though. Tonight was about getting past her upbringing. She loved her parents, but their views on sex were not hers. She was curious about kink, and tonight would give her real-life experience beyond the books she'd read. It would also help her make a decision about pursuing a relationship with Jordan.

"When we get there, once you put your things away, we'll go over the rules, and then go into the club."

"All right." She shifted in her seat.

"You're holding something back. What is it?"

"Nothing." Crystal glanced out the window. They were leaving town now. She remembered driving this road the first time she picked up Sierra at the club that fateful night Sierra met Max.

"Crystal." His tone was firm.

She sighed. "What happens if I can't handle the club?" It was a worry in the back of her mind.

He squeezed her hands. "Tonight is for you to see what goes on. If you are bothered by anything, we can leave. I don't want you to worry about it. Relax and explore.

"But what if another Dom won't take no for an answer?" Her brain had been coming up with different scenarios.

"You'll see when you get there that we have specially coded bracelets. Remember, it's all about consent. You have the right to say no."

"Safe, sane, and consensual." The words slipped from her lips.

"Right." They fell silent.

Crystal's mind kept going over the information Sierra had given her and the application itself. How would other members of the club view her? Sierra told her Thursdays weren't super busy, so she should be fine, but Crystal wasn't so sure. Damn, why was she trying to borrow trouble?

When Jordan turned, Crystal's nerves tightened. He stopped at the gate. Interesting. The night she picked up Sierra, the gate had been open. He rolled down his window and punched in a code at the call box. The gates parted, and he drove through.

The club was lit up, as she remembered. There were about a dozen cars in the parking lot. Jordan parked, and Crystal reached for the door handle.

"Stay there," he ordered as he jumped out of the vehicle. Then he was at her door, opening it and holding out his hand to help her out of the SUV. A gentleman. She'd almost forgotten what one was like.

"Thank you."

He locked his SUV, and they walked to the door. A big *WS* was carved into the door with the W and S entwined in an aqua-blue color outlined in black.

"WS?" she asked.

"Wicked Sanctuary."

Crystal brought her hand up to her mouth to stifle her laughter. What a play on words. Jordan pushed the door open and guided her into the foyer.

The man behind the desk greeted Jordan. "Good evening, Master Jordan."

"Evening, Ralph."

"Master?" Crystal muttered.

"Behave." Jordan's arm went around her waist.

"Crystal is here tonight to observe as my guest. Max cleared it."

"Yes, I have all her information right here." Ralph smiled at her. "If you would sign right here, Miss Crystal." He pointed to her name on a large journal.

Crystal signed beside her name.

"Very good. Here you go." He handed Jordan two of what looked like wristbands.

"Thank you, Ralph." He guided Crystal away from the desk as other people arrived, then through a set of double doors. Once they cleared the doors, music floated in the air. "Ladies room to your left. Go ahead and put your coat and purse in a locker." He gave her a pat on the butt.

Crystal glared at him, but his eyes danced with mischief. Darn the man. Technically they weren't on the clock, but she was here because of the case. *Oh, get honest with yourself.* She was here because she wanted to be, case or no case. She walked into the ladies room.

"It's about time," Sierra said before Crystal could even look around the room. Sierra pulled Crystal into a hug.

"I don't think we're late." Crystal looked at her friend, who was dressed in a short skirt and lacy top.

"You're not. I was anxious for you to arrive. Let's get you a locker and put your stuff inside. I can't wait to see the dress you're wearing." Sierra took her hand and dragged her over to a set of lockers.

"Breathe, Sierra." Crystal glanced around the bathroom. Well, if one could call it a bathroom. Yes, it had stalls, but also there were showers, lockers, and racks of towels and robes. "This is one heck of a bathroom."

"I know. The first time I saw it, I wondered about

it." Sierra took Crystal's purse and put it in an open locker. "Come on, I want to see your outfit."

"You've seen this dress before. It isn't new. Patience."

"Not tonight."

Crystal laughed. She undid her coat and slipped it off.

"Damn, I forgot the dress showed a lot of skin. Has Jordan seen you yet?"

"No. Too much?" Crystal thought the black cocktail dress was perfect for tonight. Yes, it showed a lot of skin. The top of the dress was cut low in the front and back, but not so low her breasts were on display. The lacy sleeves allowed the air to caress her skin.

She glanced at herself in the mirror. Actually not too much skin was showing. The skirt fell to above her knees, and as long as she was careful, she wouldn't flash anyone when she sat down.

"It's fantastic. You look super sexy."

Crystal's expression changed from anxiety to relief. . "Thank goodness." She placed her coat in the locker and started to shut it.

"Shoes," Sierra said.

"What?"

"Are you sure you want to walk around the club in heels all night?"

"It shouldn't be an issue for me." Crystal sat down on the bench. "Is there something I should know about the flooring?"

"The flooring is specially made and sanitized each night, and no food or drink is allowed in the play area. Most of the women go barefoot or in ballet type slippers. Everyone is very careful not to step on toes. But it's up to you if you want to wear them."

"Okay." Crystal adjusted the ankle strap of her shoes. "I'm going to leave them on." She didn't feel comfortable in bare feet.

"Come on, let me show you how to lock up your things, and we'll go." Sierra showed her how to lock the locker with her thumbprint, then arm-in-arm, they walked into the hallway.

Jordan was waiting, and Crystal's mouth went dry. Apparently he'd changed out of his khakis and polo. He was wearing a pair of well-fitted, low slung black jeans, black boots, and no shirt. Da-yum! The man had a six pack. His eyes widened when he saw her.

"Sierra, would you give us a minute? We'll be right in." His voice was deep and husky. A tingle shot through her body at the low rumble of his voice.

"Sure." Sierra squeezed her arm before letting go and crossing over to another set of doors. When Sierra opened them, the music grew louder, and Crystal caught a glimpse of other people.

Jordan took Crystal by the shoulders, the heat from his hands penetrating to her bones. "If I'd known what you had on under your coat, we never would have made it out of your apartment."

His tone was so husky she had to lower her lashes so he didn't see the satisfaction in her eyes at how she affected him. She'd thought long and hard last night and today. It was time to put aside her fears and let nothing stop her. She was a grown woman with feelings and desires.

"I feel like I should say I'm sorry. But I'm not." Her gaze met his. She wanted to be sexy and desirable tonight.

"Never be sorry. You are an alluring and beautiful woman. I want to get to know you." His fingers tightened on hers. "I'll have to beat the Doms off with a stick tonight."

Crystal drew in a deep breath. "Yourself included." Being able to tease Jordan was new for her, and she liked it.

"Maybe. But I have iron control."

"Oh?" What would it take for him to lose that iron control? Not tonight, she reminded herself. Tonight was to understand more about the lifestyle for the case.

"Let's go into the club before I change my mind, bundle you out to my car, take you back to my place, and ravish you." He released her shoulders and slipped his arm around her waist. "Don't forget to call me Sir."

Crystal took two steps then stopped. "From my reading, since we're not in a committed relationship or in the lifestyle, I'm not required to call you sir."

Jordan closed his eyes and then opened them. "You're right. Habit."

"But I'm not saying it might happen or not. I need to understand kink first, especially related to the case."

"Then you will make a decision if we explore our attraction to each other?"

"Yes." She was jumping into the deep end with both feet. "Don't rush me, Jordan. I still need time."

"Noted."

He opened the doors, and they walked into the club.

Crystal's eyes went wide. Books never described this. The club was huge with muted lighting. Off to her right was a bar, beyond the cubes she assumed were for storage. There was a big seating area with tables and chairs, sofas, and over-stuffed chairs.

There was a big open area in the middle. Open, but not completely. She shook her head. There were sofas and equipment in different places. To the left were raised platforms with various equipment scattered along the walls. St. Andrew's Cross, bondage table, a massage table, another with a wheel-looking thing, and yet another with a big wood structure.

"Welcome to Wicked Sanctuary," Max said, walking up to them. "I'm pleased you're here, Crystal."

"Thanks." She swallowed. Max, like Jordan, was wearing a pair of pants and shoes. Now that she thought about it, she'd barely paid attention to what anyone was wearing.

"I'll let Jordan remind you of the rules." Max looked at Jordan. "Don't forget the wristband."

"Oh yeah, thanks. I was so taken aback by what she was wearing, I forgot." Jordan reached into his pocket and pulled out two wristbands.

"If you need anything, and Jordan isn't around, find me. But I have a feeling he isn't going to leave your side." Max smiled and then left them.

"Wristbands? You mentioned them on the drive, and I saw the man at the desk give them to you."

"Yes. Remember you asked me about the questionnaire and negotiations?"

"I do." He slipped the black band on his wrist and took her left arm.

"These help Doms know the sub's interests." He slipped a white one on her wrist. "A pure white band means you're a new member and not allowed to play yet."

"Yours is black."

"It's for a club Master."

"So much terminology. I'll never remember it all."

"I don't expect you to. Not tonight. Ready?"

"As I'll ever be." *Be confident. You are in control.*

"My brave Crystal." Jordan guided her over to the first area. "Massage tables."

"Probably the most vanilla thing in here."

Jordan's husky laugh sent a quiver of awareness over her skin.

"You are learning the vocabulary. Yes and no. It is used to give massages and to help both Doms and subs relax. But it's also used for fire cupping."

Crystal tilted her head. "Fire cupping sounds dangerous."

"It's very relaxing." He guided her to the next area, which was larger. There were several pieces of equipment. "Bondage and spanking area."

She took a deep breath at the thought of being tied up and at Jordan's mercy. "How popular is this area?"

"Very. Thursday night is usually pretty light."

"Then why open the club?"

"If we have new members, this would be class night. We'd have to be here anyway, so we figured why not open. Some of our members like to come on less crowded nights."

They moved again. This area was much larger, taking up most of one wall. Crystal swallowed.

"The flogging area." Jordan nodded to a couple who were at one of the stations. "St. Andrew's crosses, bondage horses, and the wheel."

"What is the wheel? I've never seen anything like that."

"The wheel is an interesting piece of equipment." He guided her closer to it.

"It almost looks like a spider web," she said, trying to control her breathing. She hadn't expected this to be so arousing. Her skin tingled under his touch.

"Easier to catch you in my web," Jordan whispered. "Basically," he continued. "You can restrain a sub to the wheel and flog or tease. There is also a pin that allows the wheel to move, for even more fun."

The sound of something hitting flesh caused Crystal to jump and turn her head. The couple Jordan nodded to had moved to the St. Andrew's cross. The man had a flogger in his hand.

"Would you like to watch?"

"Not now." Crystal hoped her voice was steady.

"All right." He led her to the big wooden structure. "This is called a bondage system, but we refer to it as 'The Tormentor'."

This time, Crystal couldn't repress the tingles going through her body. Jordan slipped his arm around her waist and pulled her to his side.

"It was named by the subs here in the club. The wooden sections can be moved around so one can place their sub in several different poses. There are the usual stocks for neck and arms as well as cock and ball stocks."

"Ouch," she whispered.

"I'm not a sub, but they seem to like it…sometimes." He guided her away and toward the social area.

"Jordan, can we borrow you for a few minutes?" Max asked.

Jordan looked down at her. "I'm fine. I'll wait in the social area." He nodded.

Crystal noticed a beautiful woman in a leather outfit sitting in the social area. Since Jordan was in a conversation with Max and Damon, she walked over and sat down across from the woman. Her brown hair was arranged in a simple updo. The leather pants fit her like a second skin, as did the deep red corset. Her black knee length boots were magnificent.

The woman's brown eyes assessed Crystal. Oh crap, she made a mistake. This woman was no submissive, she was—what was it, oh yes—a Domme.

"My apologies," Crystal said, starting to get up.

"No please," the woman said in a soft voice. "It's okay. I saw you come in with Jordan."

"I don't want to break protocol on my first time here."

The woman laughed and several people turned their heads. "No worries. I'm Sage."

"I'm Crystal. Wait. Did you say Sage?" The name of Jordan's client.

"Yes. Is there a problem?" The laughter disappeared, and her eyes grew cold.

"No, ma'am. I work for Jordan as a paralegal; that's why he brought me here. So I could learn about the lifestyle."

Sage relaxed. "I see. Leave it to Jordan to cover all the bases. Ask me any question you want."

"Thank you. First off, tell me how you knew you were a Dominant?"

* * * *

When Sage laughed, Jordan turned his head. It had been a while since anyone made Sage laugh. He saw Crystal sitting with her and thought about going over, but Sage smiled at Crystal. They were talking. Good. That was the part of the point of tonight.

He knew Sage would be there. She'd told him she could come on Thursday nights because Brady wasn't there. He noted Sage looked lost and alone without Brady at her side.

Jordan hated he had to keep the two separated, but until they had the preliminary hearing, he didn't have a choice. Not that Brady cared about anything right now. He was as miserable as Sage was.

Jordan kept his gaze on the two women as they talked. Crystal's face was animated, and her hands moved as she talked. He was glad to see her taking the club in stride. He hadn't been too sure how she'd react. She'd asked him questions while they walked around, but nothing too detailed.

"Crystal looks like she's doing well," Damon said.

"Yeah." He looked at his friend. "You okay?"

"Peachy. Tessa shot me down again. The woman has gotten under my skin."

"I can tell." Jordan smiled. "All I can say is tread lightly. Tessa might be the quiet one, but I have a feeling she has steel in her spine. I mean that in the most flattering way. She's cute."

"She is." Damon looked around. "At least tonight is a light crowd."

"That's why I brought Crystal tonight. This way she can ask questions and explore without too many people trying to capture her attention."

"So is she going to be your sub?"

"Jury's still out." Jordan wouldn't mind if she was. Hell, he'd already told her that, but it was up to her to give her consent. Some might say her signing the employment agreement and the club paperwork was consent enough, but the two things were completely dissimilar, one having no bearing on the other. He wanted specific consent.

"Master Damon," one of the Doms said, approaching the pair. "I need some help setting up the bondage chair, and Master Jordan, if you have time, would you instruct me on how to get my sub to relax? This is her first time playing in public."

Jordan looked over at Crystal. She was deep in her conversation with Sage. She'd be safe there. "Sure."

"Thank you." The trio walked over to the bondage station and began working.

* * * *

"Much of what you've told me, I've never thought about. Thank you," Crystal said.

"Will it help you with my case?" Sage asked.

"I think it will. I need to further digest the information, but it sure seems like we're on the right side of this."

Sage reached out and captured Crystal's hands in hers. "Thank you. I feel so lost without Brady."

Crystal empathized with Sage. Sage had told her how she and Brady met and how they managed to mesh together.

"I'm going to do my best, along with Jordan, to make sure you and Brady are back together."

Sage nodded and let go of Crystal's hands.

Crystal tilted her head as she noticed a small group gathering near one of the stages. "What is going on over there?"

Sage turned in her seat. "A scene along with some instruction. Come on." Sage rose to her feet and took her by the arm. "This will help you learn more."

Before Crystal could say anything, Sage was pulling her across the room. She found an empty sofa and pushed Crystal down before sitting next to her. "I'm sure Master Jordan told you about protocol, but you don't interrupt a scene."

"Right, I remember." Crystal glanced at the stage. There was a beautiful blonde woman being restrained to a chair, and Jordan stood off to the side. What was he doing up there?

"Take your time," Jordan said, his voice clear and loud enough those close to the stage could hear.

Crystal froze. The music was still on, but much softer than before, as if it had been turned down. Interesting.

"That's it," Jordan said. "Run your fingers over her skin, touching, finding those spots that make her squirm or flush."

The woman shifted as the man ran his fingers over the top of her breasts, and it was then Crystal realized the woman was naked. Funny how, once she entered the club, she never gave a thought to how people were dressed or, in this case, not dressed.

"You like this, baby?" the man said, squeezing the woman's nipple.

"Yes, Sir."

"Help me." Crystal leaned closer to Sage and kept her voice low. "I don't understand the Sir and Master bits."

"It's a sign of respect and knowing who is in charge, like you called me ma'am."

"But why do some people refer to Jordan as Master Jordan?"

"Because he's one of the founders of the club in addition to Master Max and Master Damon."

Jordan had mentioned the three of them started the club, but he'd left out the Master part. "Got it."

The woman squealed, and Crystal turned her attention back to the stage. The man had a feather in his hand and was running it over her breasts, then down her belly and back up.

Crystal squirmed in her seat. How would the feather feel on her skin? Would Jordan torment her as this man was doing or just tease her a little bit? Both, she bet. And suddenly, she knew she wanted to find out.

She drew in a deep breath. Oh, brother. She wanted to explore kink with Jordan. Not that she hadn't been thinking about it, but now her brain lit up with *let's go for it,* and at the same time, her heart said, *Trust Jordan. Play with him.*

Crystal clamped a hand over her mouth before the laughter bubbling up escaped. Was she crazy? Not really. She wanted to explore this attraction to Jordan, and this seemed like a good way. Who knew, maybe kink was her thing?

Slut. Whore. Sinner. Her parents' voices filtered through her head, but she pushed them away. They were in the past. She controlled her life now.

"Very good, now take the next toy and run it over her skin," Jordan said.

For the next thirty minutes, Crystal watched as the Dom, with instructions from Jordan, tormented his sub. Crystal was fascinated at how the sub reacted, but also the Dom. They both seemed to be enjoying themselves.

"Please, Sir, no more. Yellow," the sub called out.

"Ah, my pet," the Dom said. "You are so ready to

go over, aren't you?"

"Yes, Sir. Please, Sir."

The Dom turned to Jordan and spoke quietly before he began to remove the restraints from his sub. Crystal almost breathed a sigh of relief. Her nipples were tight, and her clit throbbed. She was sure her thong was soaked with her own need.

"Damn, that was a good scene," someone behind Crystal said.

"Yes, Master Jordan knows his stuff," another voice said.

"Excuse me, Mistress Sage, is this your sub?" a dark haired male asked, coming up to them.

"No, she's not, but you're not paying attention, Remy." Sage gestured to where Crystal's hands rested in her lap.

"Ah, you're right, Mistress. I wasn't. Maybe next time." He wandered away.

Over the next few minutes, several men approached her and Sage only to walk away with a shake of their head.

"What the heck was that all about?" Crystal asked Sage.

"They were looking for someone to play with tonight."

Crystal shrank against the sofa, and Sage smiled.

"No worries there. The white band signifies you are not ready for playing or a scene yet."

"Thank goodness." Crystal let out a breath. She didn't want anyone but Jordan.

"Don't worry. I get the impression Jordan isn't about to let anyone take you away from him."

Crystal's head jerked up at Sage's statement. "I

didn't say anything out loud."

"No, but it's written on Jordan's face."

Crystal glanced up to see Jordan marching toward them, a frown on his face. "Mistress Sage, thank you for taking care of Crystal and talking with her."

"Any time." Sage stood. "She's a keeper. She needs some instruction though, Master Jordan." With that, Sage walked away.

Jordan sat next to Crystal so her body tilted toward him. "How did you like the scene?" He put his arm around her shoulders.

"It was interesting." Her skin vibrated at his touch. "Why were you giving instruction?"

"The Dom and his sub are newer to the club scene. She's been having trouble relaxing, so her Dom asked if I'd help him tease her until she relaxed and was on the verge of climax."

"You did that." Crystal tried not to shift in her seat. Her body was overheated.

"You're flushed." Jordan leaned over. "Are you aroused?"

Heat flooded her cheeks.

Jordan ran a finger over her hot cheek. "I'm glad you're aroused."

"Why?" The question popped out before she could stop it.

"Some women are not visual creatures like men are. Watching others doesn't always arouse them."

"Oh?" She never thought about that.

"Did Sage look aroused to you?"

Crystal tilted her head. "No, not really, but she's sad. She misses her sub."

"True. It takes a bit more than a little foreplay for

Sage to get her engines going."

Jealousy swept over Crystal. "How do you know that?" She crossed her arms over her chest.

"Easy, my little spitfire." He slipped his hand behind her neck.

Crystal inhaled at his hold on her neck, her nerves going on alert. Hell, her whole body was on alert now. Awareness and need flashed through her. His touch was firm and gentle at the same time.

"As one of the Masters of the club, it's my job to know about the members."

"You know everyone?"

"I know names, faces, and what most of them like. For example…" He glanced around the room. "See the man and woman by the bondage system?"

Thank goodness the lighting was muted so she could see. "The Tormentor?"

"Yes."

"I see them."

"That's Dom Thomas. His sub is Rose. Rose enjoys being bound, having her body played with until her Dom fucks her."

Heat flooded Crystal at Jordan's words.

"Dom Thomas wants to please his sub. He enjoys seeing her at his mercy, the cries she makes when he touches a sensitive spot."

Crystal lowered her lashes. Jordan's hand tightened on her neck. "Open your eyes and watch them for a few minutes." He waited until her eyes were open. "Notice how little touches make her vibrate, the smile that plays around his lips, the way their gazes meet."

"He's talking to her. I can see his lips moving."

"Yes. A good Dom will check in with his sub as

they're playing to make sure she's okay. He'll also watch how she's reacting to what he's doing."

"I don't understand." So many nuances.

"Like I'm watching you now."

Oh yes, he was watching her all right. The impact of his gaze caused her breathing to hiccup.

"Your breathing has increased; your skin is flushed, but there's more to it." He shifted in his seat. "Your nipples are hard, poking against your bodice, and I bet if I slipped my hand between your legs, I'd find you're wet."

She tightened her abs and pressed her legs together.

"See there. You reacted to my words."

Damn it! He was right; she did. "Jordan—"

"We're not on the clock. We're two people in a club, exploring."

While his words inflamed her, this wasn't the place or time. Some might argue with her, but they barely knew each other. She twisted in his hold and placed her hands against his chest. "Yes, we are two people exploring, but for professional purposes. You haven't earned the right to more—yet."

Crystal swallowed. This was so overwhelming, both mentally and physically. She'd never reacted to a man this way before, not even to her boyfriends in college.

His lips turned up. "I will earn the right. I can promise you that." He loosened his hold on her, and her breathing eased. "Are you ready to leave?"

She blinked. "Leave? Oh, yes. Please." She needed time to digest everything she'd seen. And to deal with the want and need flowing through her.

"Let's go say good-bye to Max and Sierra." Jordan stood and pulled her to her feet. He kept his arm around her waist as they said good night.

Crystal went into the ladies' room and retrieved her things, then met Jordan by the front door. Thank goodness he'd pulled on a t-shirt and changed into loafers. Once they were inside his vehicle and on their way, her brain began working again.

Maybe that wasn't right. It had been working, but more on a sensual level than a logical level. Now her logic was kicking back in.

"I think I have a plan of attack for Sage's case," she said as he pulled out onto the main road.

"We're off the clock. No shop talk."

"But…" He reached over and put his hand on her bare knee since her coat was open. Crystal swallowed.

"Not tonight. Relax while I drive you home." He removed his hand.

Easy for him to say. A single touch from him made her body sit up and go "let's play". Crystal stared out the window. She had to figure out a way to handle this attraction. If a single touch did that to her, what would a kiss or an intimate caress do?

Wait a second. He'd already kissed her. If one could call a quick brush of the lips a kiss. What if he gave her one of those deep, penetrating, sensual kisses she'd read about. Her body heated. She shifted in her seat to calm her throbbing clit.

This was so unfair. She wasn't a virgin, and she wasn't as closed up as her family wanted her to be. Ice filled her veins at the thought of her family. How many times had their remonstrances and condemnation filled her with shame? Even the most innocent of actions could mean hours in the sin closet. And even now, when Crystal's life was her own, she could feel them passing judgment over her.

Thank goodness they were still in Kansas. She lit out of there the second she turned eighteen, no longer willing to live under the thumb of their warped beliefs.

She talked to her parents around the holidays, but that was about it. She hadn't visited them in years, mainly because, on her one trip back, after she graduated with her degree, they tried to convince her a woman with a job was a sign of the devil at work.

Crystal had smiled and left for home. Her home. She loved her parents, but she wouldn't allow them to control her life. Not like her brothers and sisters. Her siblings still lived in the same town and followed their parents' example. How the heck she had four brothers and three sisters was a mystery. Then again, maybe not. Her parents considered sex outside of wedlock a sin.

Sometimes she missed her family, but she had friends here. Sierra and Tessa.

"Crystal." A touch on her shoulder caused her to jump. "Sorry," Jordan said. "You were lost in thought. We're at your apartment building."

"Oh." So they were. "Sorry." She reached for the door handle.

"Sit there." Jordan opened his door, came around to hers, and helped her out of his SUV and locked it.

"I'm fine making it to my apartment," she said.

"My mother raised me to escort a woman to her front door." He cupped her elbow.

"Your mother raised a gentleman." She loved his manners. Old-fashioned, some might say, but she didn't mind. They were real manners, not the faked ones because your family told you to be nice.

When they got to her apartment, Crystal opened the door. Jordan entered, turned on the lights, and looked around before he allowed her to enter. She shook her head.

"Why did you check out my apartment?"

"To make sure you were safe." He snagged her around the waist and drew her to him. "Until tomorrow." He paused. "I want to kiss you. Is that okay, my beautiful Crystal?"

"Yes," she whispered. She wanted to taste him.

He lowered his head.

Their lips met. Crystal melted against him when his tongue brushed over her lips. Then her lips parted. He tasted of mint as their tongues tangled and dueled with each other.

Her breathing stuttered as he pulled her tighter against him, and his erection pressed against her leg.

"So damn beautiful," he whispered as he broke the kiss. "Lock the door behind me, and don't worry about what time you come into the office tomorrow." Jordan released her, grabbed the door, and shut it behind him.

Crystal stood there.

"Lock the door, Crystal."

His voice snapped her back to reality. She locked the door, then placed her palms against it. She heard his footsteps recede as he walked down the hallway. Then she placed her fingers against her throbbing lips.

She wanted more. Another kiss. A caress. Let the devil take her. She wanted everything Jordan would give her and more.

Chapter Five

Crystal walked into the office at eight Friday morning, coffee and food in hand. Valerie was already at her desk.

"You are a blessing, Crystal," Valerie said when Crystal set a cup of coffee and a muffin on her desk.

"I don't think everyone would agree with that." She grinned. "Jordan in yet?"

"He called me this morning. A court date got changed, so he's in court. He said he'd send you an email."

"Okay." Crystal went into her office and sat down. She sipped her coffee while her computer booted up, then she opened her email program and found the email from Jordan. She opened it.

Crystal, I got called into court today. I have no idea if I'll make it to the office this afternoon. Do what research you can. I've emailed a list of professionals you can speak with. Also check your text messages.

Text messages? Crystal fished her phone out of her purse. Yep, there were three text messages from

Jordan and one from Sierra.

> ***Jordan:*** *Stuck in court. How are you today?*
>
> ***Jordan:*** *Okay, you're not answering. I hope you're not upset with me. I can still taste your kiss from last night.*
>
> ***Jordan:*** *Looks like I might be here all day. Dinner tonight? Dang, they're calling me in. Text me back.*

Crystal smiled. Dinner sounded good. She'd made her decision about Jordan and how she wanted to proceed with him.

> **Crystal:** *Jordan, not upset at all. I still had my phone on silent from last night. Dinner tonight? Sure. Let me know where so I know how to dress. I'm pretty casual today since it's Friday.*

Next she opened the text message from Sierra.

> ***Sierra****: Hey, tried calling you but got voice mail. We didn't get to talk much last night. Give me a call. Maybe we can do a girls' day on Sunday and catch up. BTW – You were the talk of all the Doms last night.*

What? All the Doms were talking about her? She punched Sierra's number.

"It's about time," Sierra said.

"I'd forgotten I put my phone on silent. What do

you mean I was the talk of the Doms last night?" Crystal wasn't sure if this was a good thing or bad thing.

Sierra laughed. "You impressed a lot of them."

"How?" She thought back to last night. "I didn't do much but sit with Sage."

"That was it. The Doms have seen how sad Sage has been without Brady. You got Sage to smile and laugh."

Crystal's lips tilted up. "Sage is a nice person. She helped me understand a lot last night."

Sierra laughed again. "Don't ever tell Sage to her face. I've seen her wield a flogger, and all I can say is *ouch*."

"I bet." Sage was in excellent shape. "Look, I need to get to work."

"Okay, but we've got to figure out a girls' night. I want to know more about you and Jordan."

"Bye." Crystal pushed the off button on her phone. She loved her best friend, but she wasn't ready to discuss Jordan yet. It was all still too new.

Crystal shook her head. *Okay, put last night, the club, and Jordan out of your head; you have work to do.* She opened the list of professionals Jordan sent her.

The plan she'd thought of last night started to make more sense. She printed out the list, then picked up her phone. Time to make some calls and see if anyone had dealt with something like this before.

* * * *

Jordan rubbed the back of his neck. What a long day. It was after five. The courts never moved fast when you wanted them to, and today was one of those days. They'd barely gotten a half-hour for lunch.

He'd texted Crystal that whatever she wore to

work would be fine for dinner, and he'd pick her up at six. Damn. He wanted to cook her dinner, but there wasn't enough time for him to shop, and by the time he got anything ready, it would be after seven.

> ***Jordan:*** *Crystal, would you mind dinner at my house?*

His fingers drummed on the steering wheel as he waited for her reply.

> **Crystal:** *Sure. Do you want me to meet you at your place?*
> ***Jordan:*** *No, I'll pick you up. I'm going to order Chinese food, any objections?*
> **Crystal:** *Sounds delicious.*

Jordan grinned.

He called his favorite Chinese restaurant and placed an order to be picked up. He didn't know what Crystal liked yet, so he ordered a variety. After a quick stop to grab the food, he headed to her apartment.

Crystal was waiting outside for him. He frowned when he pulled up. She opened the door and hopped in.

"Why are you waiting outside?"

Her eyebrows rose at his tone, but he didn't care. "Because it was easier than making you park, come up and get me. Relax." She leaned over and brushed a kiss over his cheek. Then she sniffed. "That Chinese food smells delicious."

Jordan smiled. "It does. I wanted to cook for you, but I got stuck in court." He waited until she fastened her seatbelt before he pulled away from her apartment building.

"You don't need to cook for me, and you should have canceled. You must be tired."

"It was a long day." He reached over and captured her hand in his. "But I wanted to see you." Jordan glanced over at her as they reached a red light. A light blush graced her cheeks. His fingers tightened around hers. "How did your research go today?"

"Great. I talked with two different kink-friendly psychologists."

The light turned green, and he drove as she explained to him what the psychologists told her and how she thought they could utilize them and their information to help Sage.

"You know, for every expert we put on the stand, they'll put two who will deny what ours said." He pulled into his driveway.

"I know. I'm trying to figure out how we can use this to our advantage. Having information will help."

He hopped out and opened her door, reached in and got the bags of food, and led her inside. Jordan disarmed his alarm system and headed for the kitchen with Crystal following.

"Set the food down, and I'll get it all set up while you go change," she said as they walked into the kitchen.

"Giving orders, are we?" He grinned at her.

"If you're anything like me after a day in court, you want nothing better than to change into comfortable clothes."

"So true." He dropped a kiss on her nose and jogged to his bedroom. Jordan changed quickly, and by the time he returned, Crystal had set the table in the nook and had the food out.

"Were you expecting more people than the two of us?" she asked.

"No. Why?" He walked over to the fridge. "What's your poison for tonight. Beer, wine, soda, water?"

"Soda please. You bought enough food to feed five people."

Jordan set her soda on the table and held her chair out for her. He caught a whiff of strawberries as she sat down. "I wasn't sure what you liked, so I got a little bit of everything."

"I'm not a picky eater." She picked up the fried rice and put some on her plate. "Excellent assortment, by the way. Everything looks yummy."

"What we don't eat now we can have as a midnight snack."

"And what makes you think I'll still be here?"

"I'm being hopeful."

"Where did you grow up?" he asked as he dished up his food. Her fork froze on the way to her mouth.

"Kansas." She took a bite and set her fork down.

"A long way from Washington." Her smooth forehead creased into a frown. Had he hit a sore spot?

"Yes." Crystal glanced out the window and then back at him. "I left home at eighteen and headed west. I ended up in Seattle. My first job was as a waitress. I'm so not cut out for that type of work, but my boss took pity on me. He gave me a hostess job because I was friendly. It worked out."

Interesting. While a lot of kids left home at eighteen, she'd traveled thousands of miles with no plans. He was curious about what made her leave her family. "Why did you become a paralegal?"

"People from a nearby law firm came in for lunch every Friday. I'd hear bits and pieces as they waited for their table. It sounded fascinating. One day I talked to one of the paralegals, and she helped me figure out which college to attend and what classes to take."

"You never thought about college before then?" She was bright and sharp; why wouldn't she have considered college?

"No." She let out a sigh. "My parents didn't believe in anything beyond high school. I wasn't allowed to take my SATs or any placement tests for college. They expected me to get married and have children."

Jordan pushed his empty plate away and took a sip of his beer. His childhood had been good until right before his eighteenth birthday. The day his father killed his mother. "Do you have any brothers and sisters?"

Crystal gave a bitter laugh. "Four brothers and three sisters. We're all a little over a year apart. I have two older brothers and one older sister, then two younger brothers and two younger sisters."

"Middle child."

"Yeah, pretty much."

"Are your brothers and sisters still in Kansas?"

"As far as I know. I don't have a lot of contact with them."

Interesting that she didn't have a lot of contact. He glanced at her plate; she'd barely eaten. "I'm an only child."

"I'm not sure it was any better than having lots of siblings." She picked up her fork and began eating again.

"I wasn't lonely. I had lots of friends, and my mom was the best." He allowed himself to remember his mother's bright smile and how it would fade when his father's temper got out of control and he would yell. But his father never hit his mother until the day his father killed her. "She was a stay-at-home mom. Sometimes I can still smell her oatmeal raisin cookies she baked when I was little."

"Was this your parents' house?"

"No. My childhood home was demolished years ago." He'd seen to it when he finally had the money. He bought it from the foreclosure company and then leveled it, hoping to bury the ghosts of his past.

"I'm sorry."

"I'm not." He took a long drink of his beer as she stared at him. "My father killed my mother in that house." His gut clenched. He rarely talked about his family, but if he was going to have a relationship with Crystal, he wanted to be open and honest.

"What? Oh my God, Jordan." She stood up, crossed over to him, and stood behind his chair. She leaned down and hugged him from behind. "I'm so sorry."

The strangle-hold on his heart eased. "Thank you." He didn't know what else to say. He reached up and put his hands on her arms, enjoying the warmth of her touch. It had been a while since he'd allowed anyone this close to him, not counting his friends. He took a deep breath and quickly changed the subject. "If you're finished eating, let's put the extra food away and go into the family room."

"Sure." She released him, and he missed her warmth, but he hoped to have her in his arms soon enough.

They made short work of cleaning up and were in the family room in no time.

"I think we both had some tragedies in our childhoods," she said standing next to the sofa.

"Yes." Before she could sit down, he snagged her around the waist, and when he sat, he pulled her into his lap. He wanted to get off their childhoods and onto something more pleasant.

"Jordan," she wiggled. "This might not be a good idea."

"It's perfect. We're not on the clock, and I want to talk about us." He took a breath. "So, how do you feel about kink now that you've gone to the club?"

Her cheeks flamed. "I think I'd rather talk about your family."

"Later." He dipped his head, nuzzling her hair away from her ear. Yeah, he was using sex as a diversion, but he wanted to put his past back in the box and leave it there. "I want to talk about the club. About us."

She sighed. "Are you sure this is a good idea?" she asked.

"What? Talking about the club or the fact you're in my lap?"

"Both."

"Yes." He stared at her. "I meant what I said about my attraction to you. And last night at the club… Crystal, I'd like you to be my sub." He kept his gaze on her face.

She closed her eyes and huffed. "Tell me what being your sub would entail."

At least she wasn't shutting him down. "You've never been a sub before, correct?

"No."

"Have you ever played before?"

"Not really."

Interesting. Not a complete answer. "Clarify for me please." Her cheeks turned pink, but she held his gaze.

"When I first came to Seattle, I dated a couple of guys, and we decided to try kink."

"What happened?" The Seattle scene could be intense.

"Nothing bad. I wasn't into what they were doing." She squirmed on his lap.

"Tell me more." He'd read her limits. Nothing stood out from what he would expect from someone who was new to kink.

"After a few dates, the first guy wanted me to parade around naked when we were alone together. Not my thing. So he was done, and I walked away." She shivered. "The second guy I dated was a sadist. I'm not into pain, so he only lasted another few dates."

"Not the best Doms for you." He rubbed her shoulders. She was tense. "How did you meet them?"

"Online." She paused, clearly considering her next words. "Well, the first two, at least. The last one was a piece of work. Him, I didn't meet online."

She was so stiff. Jordan didn't like making her relive something she reacted to this way, but he needed to understand. "What happened?" Crystal opened her mouth then closed it. "Why the hesitation?" he asked.

"This one is hard to talk about." She drew in a breath. "I know this will stay between us." She glanced up at him.

"Naturally, unless the man did something to hurt you, then all bets are off."

"So protective," she said with a small smile.

"Of you, yes." He wasn't going to lie to her.

"Because you've seen my resume, you know which law firm I worked with before I went freelance."

"I do." Why did he have a feeling this was why she insisted on the clause in the employment contract saying her job was safe.

"So, I was dating one of the lawyers there. Which is why I'm wary of us having a relationship. Nothing heavy, we enjoyed dinners out and stuff like that. I don't know how we got to talking on the subject of sex and kink." A vibration shook her body. "Anyway, he said he'd always wanted to try kink, and I was willing to give it a go."

Many started off being curious. "What went wrong?"

She scoffed. "Everything. He showed up to my apartment dressed in red leather pants, a black shirt, and steel-toed boots. Then he wanted me to wear an outfit that, shall we say, was more revealing than I would wear. That was the first fight."

"The outfit you wore to the club was pretty daring." The dress fit her perfectly and showed off her long legs.

"Yes, I'm more confident in myself now than I was then, and with you, I knew nothing was going to happen unless I wanted it." She took a breath. "I dressed a little more conservatively, and he took me to a club." Crystal snorted.

"By your reaction I'm guessing not a good club?"

"It wasn't as good as Wicked Sanctuary, and certainly not one I would have chosen, especially in Seattle. We got there, and he got all bossy and shit—and not in a good way." She let out a nervous laugh. "I was nervous and scared, but he was acting so out of character

I was hard-pressed not to laugh in his face. He had no clue about the lifestyle, and all I knew was from reading. I began thinking it was a bad idea."

"Was there consent?" It was one of the biggest mistakes people made, even him a time or two.

"I said yes to going to the club, so he felt he had the right to boss me around." She gazed up at him. "We got into an argument at the club, and he tried to force me to play. I started screaming red, and the monitors came flying."

"I'm glad you called out the safe word."

"Me too. He got upset. Tried to tell the dungeon monitors it was a minor argument between us, but they didn't believe him. They asked me if I had a way home. I said I didn't, that we had come together."

"What happened?" He hoped the monitors were good guys.

"He stood there all smug, saying he wasn't going to leave. One of the DMs smiled and took me by the arm. He told me he'd call me a cab, and we walked away. I got home and went to bed, putting it out of my mind."

"But that wasn't the end of it?" He'd met the type before. Ones who believed they were the perfect Dom, and no one should defy them.

"No. When I got to the office the next morning, I was getting funny looks from everyone. I'd barely settled at my desk when I was called into the managing partner's office. I knew what was coming from the look on his face. They were letting me go. He indicated they would make it look like I decided to resign so as not to cause any issue."

"That's bullshit." What the hell was wrong with that firm?

"Yes, but I didn't want to make waves. I knew better than to date someone I worked with. I'm not excusing what happened, but it did give me the guts to go out on my own." She smiled then, the first real smile Jordan had seen from her since she began her story. "The partners all gave glowing recommendations."

"They should have." If she'd wanted to make waves, she had one hell of a lawsuit. "What happened to the guy?"

"Nothing. I found out as I was packing up my desk he'd blabbed to everyone that he saw me at the club, naked and playing with some biker dudes. All untrue of course, but this was a conservative firm."

"Yet he got to keep his job." Damn, he hated the double standard society put on women.

"He did." She gave him a little smile. "Although I heard through the grapevine he put the moves on a client and was fired a few months later."

"Good." He brushed his lips over her temple. "Now I understand the whole thing in the employment contract."

"Yes." She sighed. "As for being your sub. I want to try, but I have limits."

"I'm listening." Jordan tapped down his inner joy at her agreement to being his sub.

"This stays outside the office. Nothing while we're working."

"Agreed," he said.

"I trust you won't brag to anyone."

"Of course not." He would never do that to a woman. "This is between us. But you do realize Max, Damon, and Sierra will know."

"Yes, they're part of the club. Tessa will also

know. I can't keep this from her."

Jordan nodded. "You read and signed the NDA for the club, so no worries there."

"I'm also guessing I'll need to fill out the questionnaire?"

"Yes. We can do it tomorrow."

"Perfect." She leaned her head against his shoulder. "I'll make mistakes," she whispered.

"So will I. No relationship is perfect." He'd screwed up before. "Here's one thing I think we can both agree on. In the club or in the bedroom, you will call me Sir or Master, your choice."

"Okay." She sighed, and her body relaxed against his.

Good, he wanted her relaxed. "What you wore to the club Thursday night was fine, but I would prefer something that gives me better access to your breasts."

"I have the perfect outfit."

Crystal smiled and snuggled closer to him, enjoying the feel of each other, for a while. Jordan glanced down at his new sub. Her eyes were closed, and her breathing was calm and even. His Crystal had fallen asleep, in his arms no less. He grinned and shifted so he could rest his arm on the sofa arm.

He wouldn't mind a little nap. Maybe when they woke, Crystal would be up to a little fun.

* * * *

Bright sunshine warmed Crystal's face, and she frowned. Had she'd forgotten to close the shade last night? She reached for a pillow to cover her head so she could go back to sleep. Her hand encountered a warm, hard body.

What? She opened her eyes, and her breath caught

in her throat. She was in bed with a man. She carefully raised her head. Oh my God, not just any man. Jordan. She remembered them having dinner last night and talking, then…she must have fallen asleep.

How did one handle this? She'd never woken up in a man's bed before. She shifted, but his arm tightened around her, and one of his legs shifted over hers.

She didn't mind being in his arms, now that she thought about it. The warmth of his body against hers made her nerves tingle. She could lie here in his arms and enjoy the moment, couldn't she?

She could. No one was stopping her, and since he was asleep, maybe she could explore a little bit. Her gaze roamed over Jordan's face. He looked relaxed for once, and there was a hint of stubble. How would it feel against her skin?

Unable to help herself, she ran a finger over his jaw and bit back a giggle. His stubble tickled her skin. She continued her journey with her finger, over his strong chin, to his temple, enjoying the feel of his skin beneath hers.

"Feeling frisky this morning?" Languid brown eyes stared at her.

"Good morning," she said.

"It is." He shifted, and the next thing she knew, his mouth covered hers.

She stiffened. She probably had morning breath, but then he probably did too. His tongue traced her lips, and she parted them, relaxing into him.

Their tongues dueled with each other. He rolled her onto her back, and she pulled him to her. His hair-roughened chest rubbed against her breasts. Her brain kicked in. She broke the kiss.

"How did I get naked?"

"You're not." He placed soft kisses across her cheek. "You still have your panties on, but I can easily take care of them." His hand slipped to her hip under the sheet.

"Jordan." Why did it come out as a plea rather than a rebuke? Maybe because she wanted him to touch her.

"Yes, sweetheart?" His fingers slipped beneath the band of her panties. "I undressed you last night because I didn't want you to be uncomfortable."

He brushed the top of her mound, and she froze. Was he going to touch her intimately? Yep. Her lashes slid closed as he stroked her outer pussy lips. Her hips shifted. Oh God, she wanted him to touch her.

"Crystal." He said her name softly, and she opened her eyes. "Yes or no, sweetheart?"

Yes or no? What was he asking? Then she realized, he wasn't going to go any further without her consent. Damn, that was sexy. "Yes, please," she whispered. The hell with everything. She wanted this. She wanted Jordan.

Jordan pushed up on one arm and flung the sheet off himself and onto her. Crystal swallowed when she saw his cock. He was hard and pulsing. The man looked like a sexy god.

"If I'm going to do this, I'm going to do it my way." He placed a kiss on her lips before he slid down the bed, taking the sheet with him to expose more of her.

Crystal shifted her legs as he continued his journey. This was crazy. But was it? Her body heated under Jordan's gaze. Her nipples grew hard, and her pussy pulsed with need.

"We're in the bedroom," he said to her as he maneuvered his body and pushed open her legs so he fit between them.

"Yes, Sir." Her voice was soft and tentative.

Jordan's eyes flashed with desire and heat. "My dick is like steel, hearing that word from your lips." He leaned down and kissed her belly, before he slid his fingers under her panties and ripped them.

"Hey!" she protested.

"I'll buy you more," he promised as he tossed the ruined fabric across the room, then slid his finger over her mound.

Her core clenched at the feel of his slightly rough skin against her most sensitive area. He didn't stop and dipped one finger into her pussy, pulled it out, and slipped it into his mouth.

Her eyes widened, and he grinned at her. "Sweet and salty. You taste good."

Heat flooded her veins, and she closed her eyes. No man had ever tasted her. Before she could tell Jordan it wasn't necessary, his lips were against her mound. "Jordan…Sir…No."

He didn't listen to her. His fingers parted her pussy lips, and his tongue dived in.

Oh dear Lord. Crystal barely prevented her hips from leaving the mattress as she found his head and tangled her fingers in his hair. His head rose, and she sighed. Oh good, he wasn't going to continue.

"Raise your hands above your head." His voice was husky and rough.

She stared at him. "Arms above your head." This time there was more of a command behind the words, and Crystal did as he said. This thrust her chest up a bit, but also made her feel vulnerable.

"Good girl," he whispered before he lowered his head once again.

Crystal's fingers curled into her palms as he licked and nipped at her pussy. Jordan seemed to enjoy himself, and she was happy. Who was she kidding? She was delirious with pleasure.

When his tongue flicked her clit, she moaned as the little bundle of nerves throbbed in excitement. She fought to keep her arms above her head as he asked. Her reaction to him wasn't what she expected. Crystal didn't feel shy or ashamed with Jordan. Her moan must have encouraged him, because he continued to play with her clit as he slipped a finger into her pussy. Her walls contracted against the digit.

He added a second finger and sucked on her clit. The more he moved his fingers in and out of her pussy, the more her muscles tightened. Crystal's arms shifted. No, she had to keep them above her head, but his mouth on her pussy woke every nerve in her body. Her nerves tingled with need.

Her clit pulsed harder with each pass of his tongue. She wanted more. She wanted everything he could give her. Her toes curled as he hit a sweet spot with his fingers. A quiver started in her stomach.

"Sir, I'm going to come." She was flying high already from his touch. She wasn't going to be able to hold back.

His gaze met hers, and she could feel him smile against her before he went back to licking, sucking, and fingering her.

Oh damn! The tingles in her toes began working their way up her body. With each lick and slide of his fingers, her muscles contracted more and more, and then…her pussy clenched. She couldn't catch her breath. Her body quivered with hot tendrils of her release.

Jordan didn't stop. He kept stroking her until her orgasm settled down, then he lifted his head and climbed up her body. "You taste so sweet when you come."

His lips captured hers. Crystal tasted her own spices on his lips, and she didn't mind the flavor. Their tongues tangled together until he lifted his head.

"Now that's a fun way to wake up." His breath played against her cheek.

Slut. Whore. The words struck from out of nowhere. Crystal stiffened and wiggled beneath him. She needed to get out of this bed. Now! "If you don't mind, I need to go to the bathroom." She stifled the panic racing through her body.

"By all means." He rolled away from her. Crystal sprang from the bed and then looked at him. She had no idea where the bathroom was.

"The door on the right." He gestured to it.

"Thank you." She ran for the bathroom. Somehow she managed to shut the door behind her and not slam it. What had she done?

Crystal placed her hands on the sink and stared at herself in the mirror. Nothing different. Oh, her face was flushed and her hair mussed, but nothing otherwise to tell anyone what had happened between her and Jordan.

Jezebel.

Get out of my head. She wanted to scream the words. This was so unfair. She was enjoying Jordan's loving. Why couldn't she stop the voices? Maybe she needed to see a psychologist again?

She took a deep breath and let it out. Then did it

again. With each breath, her nerves stopped twitching. *Get your act together.* What she and Jordan had done was consensual and downright sexy. She had nothing to be ashamed of. They were both adults. Her body quivered with need.

His touch was so gentle and made her feel so special. Her body craved his touch. She lifted her head.

"I am a grown woman, and I decide what I do," she said out loud at her reflection.

* * * *

Jordan couldn't stop smiling. Crystal was a treasure. She'd been a little hesitant when he ordered her to put her hands over her head, but she'd done it and kept them there even as he brought her to climax.

Damn, she tasted sweet. She really did. And so responsive. He wondered when she last had a climax. Maybe it was something they should talk about over breakfast. He glanced at the bathroom door, then rose and headed down the hall. He'd use the guest bathroom.

Once he was done, he went back into his bedroom. The bathroom door was still closed. He grabbed his robe out of the closet and set it on the bed before knocking on the door. "There's a robe on my bed for you. I'm going to go start some coffee."

"Sounds good." Her voice was muffled by the door.

Jordan hesitated. Was she okay? "Is everything okay?"

"I'm fine. Just getting my bearings."

He placed his hand against the bathroom door. What could he say? "Don't be long."

"I won't."

After leaving the bedroom, he fought his instincts

as they screamed at him to go into the bathroom and check on Crystal, but he also had a feeling she needed time to process what had happened. After starting the coffee, Jordan opened the fridge. Let's see… What could he cook for her breakfast? At the sound of footsteps, he peered over the top of the refrigerator door.

He blinked. Crystal looked lost. Her green eyes were large. The white robe brought out the color in her face, and he could see the slight tremor shook her body.

Jordan closed the fridge door before walking over to her and putting his hands on her shoulders. "What is it?" he asked. Had he scared her?

"I…" She closed her eyes, then opened them. "I'm not sure how to handle this morning after stuff."

Jordan laughed. "You sit down and have some coffee while I cook you breakfast." Is that what she was worried about?

She blinked at him. "Before I do that, I have a confession to make."

"What is that, my sweet?"

"I've never had anyone do what you did to me this morning." Her cheeks were bright red by the time she stopped talking.

"Did you like it?" He hadn't thought about it being the first time she had a man go down on her. She'd been so responsive to his touch and his lips.

Her cheeks turned a deeper red. "Yes."

"Then everything is fine." He ran his finger over her hot cheek. "The men in your life didn't deserve you. I believe we're going to have a lot of first times for you while we're together." He placed a kiss on her nose and started to step back.

"One more thing," she said, and he stared at her.

"Can you please put something on? I can't eat breakfast with you naked."

Jordan's belly laugh filled the room. "As my sweet wishes." Happiness flowed through him as he pulled on his sweats and jogged out of the bedroom a moment later. Crystal wasn't running. A very good start.

At breakfast, he found out a little more about her family. She'd been brought up by very strict and religious parents. Anger and compassion filled him at her tale. It amazed him how open she was about sex. "Are you still willing to be my sub?" Jordan asked.

Crystal took a sip of her coffee. "Yes. I want to learn what it means to be your sub but also to have a relationship with you."

A sense of peace flowed over him. He'd been a little worried she might have changed her mind since last night. "I want that as well."

"So what do we do now?" she asked as she took her empty plate to the sink.

"We talk." He followed suit with his plate and cup. "Your choice. We can talk in the family room, outside on the deck, or in my home office."

She tilted her head. "Family room. Neither of us is dressed to be outside."

"We would have total privacy, but your call." He guided her to the sofa, and they both sat down. "What kind of questions do you have?"

Crystal smiled. "A lot. How did you get interested in kink?"

"I think it was always there." He shifted his body against the soft leather. "I enjoyed being with women, being in control in the bedroom."

"When did you start?"

"Are you asking me when I lost my virginity?" Her cheeks turned pink, and Jordan let go a husky laugh. "It's okay. I was sixteen."

"I was twenty."

"That doesn't surprise me, based on what you told me about your family." Unable to help himself, he ran his finger over her cheek. "How is it you're so open about sex?"

Her lashes concealed her expressive eyes from him. "I've always been curious. I had to be very careful around my family, but I did a lot of reading. Once I was on my own, I wanted to learn what I was missing. Continue with your story."

"During my senior year in high school, I started becoming aware of my dominant tendencies. It was more than sex. I did it in sports as well. One of my coaches noticed it on the soccer field, so he took me aside and discussed what being a Dominant meant."

"But you were underage."

Jordan laughed. "He talked about it in general, not in a sexual context, not until I was over eighteen." He closed his eyes and took a breath. "I told you my father killed my mother."

"Yes." Her hand touched his.

Jordan turned his hand over, and their fingers entwined. "My dad had a temper, but until that day, he hadn't hurt my mother or me. We were kind of used to his verbal rages."

"Still, it doesn't excuse what he did."

"No, it doesn't." He couldn't forgive his father for what he'd done. Even after all these years. "I worried I'd inherited his temper."

"I can see why you might worry."

Jordan was happy she didn't feed him platitudes. "I went a little out of control after his trial. I could tell my own anger was spilling over into other aspects of my life. I was still in contact with my soccer coach, so he offered to help me."

"What did he do?"

"Helped me channel my negative emotions. He taught me how to be a Dominant and remain in control of my emotions. Not only in the kink community, but with action. He introduced me to a friend who taught me to box."

"How did he teach you? He didn't hurt you, did he?"

"Sweet Crystal." He squeezed her hand. "No, he didn't hurt me. He knew people in the community and introduced me. It was the best thing for me. They taught me what it means to be a good Dominant and what it meant in terms of sexual situations and non-sexual situations."

"I'm glad someone helped you."

"I am too. The more I learned, the more I found a place where I belonged."

"Have you had a sub before?"

"Not a sub, but a bottom." He wasn't going to lie to her. "But not in the same way I want you to be my sub."

"Explain please, because I'm confused."

"The term submissive can be distinguished as either a submissive, which usually implies a D/s committed relationship, like Max and Sierra, or bottom – a submissive who is not in a committed relationship, is interested in only casual play. I've played with bottoms at the club or a party, but there is nothing outside of play. I never brought them to my home."

"Oh." Her eyes grew wide.

"I'm not going to say I didn't play at the club, but nothing beyond a willing bottom at the club who is unattached. I'll refer to subs as we talk since it's easier. And I've never had sex with a bottom."

"No sex." Her voice was soft.

"That's right. I was waiting for you."

Her cheeks turned red. "But there's no way you would know I was going to come into your life."

"True. But you did."

Crystal shook her head. "Crazy man. Can you tell me more about how you, Max, and Damon came to be partners in Wicked Sanctuary?"

"We met during a munch and hit it off. We would meet for dinner or drinks but also at the parties. We were tired of hooking up with different subs at parties. Max came up with the idea of a private club. He had the land, so we started planning."

"You said you were partners."

"Yep. Max put up the majority of the money, which is why he runs it. Damon and I put up some money, but we mainly do other duties. I help teach the classes for new members. Damon is almost always in the club as a dungeon monitor when it's open."

"Sounds like it's become a good partnership."

"It is. We were friends before Max even thought of the club, and now we're even closer. The club has been a dream come true."

"A good outlet for men like you, Max, and I'm guessing Damon to allow their dominant side out without worrying how society is going to view you."

"That's a very enlightened statement." Crystal

was a smart cookie, and she was willing to talk with him.

"I have been reading, and from what I saw on Thursday and talking with Sage, the Doms are all… What's the word? Overwhelming, but caring."

Jordan laughed. "Overwhelming is a good one, and yes, we care." He cupped her cheek. "Dominance isn't about force; it's about control. I get off on how my actions can make a sub quiver with excitement and need."

"Not fear?"

"Never fear. If I see a sub is afraid, I stop, and we talk. I'm not into pain or humiliation."

"I'm glad. I'm not either."

"I didn't think you would be." He pulled back. "Let me go get a questionnaire from my office so we can go over it."

"You keep one at home?" She blinked at him.

"Yes. Never know when it might come in handy." He stood. It took him a few minutes to get the questionnaire, paper, and a pen from his office.

"Are you ready?" he asked.

"No." Crystal turned to him.

Jordan placed everything on the table and took Crystal's hands between his. He frowned at how cold her hands were. "What is it?"

"I…" Her chin dropped. "This isn't easy for me."

Something was way off. "What happened in the few minutes I was away?"

"My parents." She let out a heavy sigh. "I've told you how I grew up and their feelings around sex."

"Yes."

"It seems like I can't get rid of those old tapes in my head."

"Sweetheart." Jordan shifted on the sofa, pulling

Crystal to his side. "Based on what you told me, I'm surprised you're as open about sex as you are. Most would still be virgins in hiding."

"So not me." She gave a little laugh. "I couldn't wait to break their bonds."

"While your parents tried to stifle your sensuality, you somehow didn't let them." He squeezed her shoulder. "You buried it deep until it was the right time."

"And now is the right time?"

"What do you think?" He was going to let her figure this out with some nudging. He was fighting his instinct to fix it. If they were going to play together and have a relationship, she needed to understand herself.

She tilted her head back and stared at him. "I'm afraid of making mistakes."

"Don't be. In new relationships, mistakes are bound to happen. Here's the thing—we need to keep the lines of communication open. If I start to overwhelm you, you tell me. Get in my face if I'm not listening."

"Yet here we sit, talking."

"Yep." He smiled.

"Okay, let's get to the questionnaire, but before we do, I have a confession to make."

"Oh?" Her cheeks turned pink again, and he was curious what she was going to confess.

"The day in the office when you gave me the questionnaire, I called Sierra, and we went over it."

"Did you check things off?"

"Yes and no." The color in her cheeks deepened. "It was mainly so I understood what the questions meant, but I did put check marks next to some things."

He nodded. "Then this should go faster."

"You're not angry?"

"Why would I be? You took the initiative even when you were unsure of a relationship with me. I'm glad you did it and talked with Sierra." He leaned forward and retrieved the questionnaire and a pen. "Okay, first question—bondage."

"Yes," she whispered.

"Any limits on what is used to bind you?"

"I don't think so."

"All right." He made some notes. "What about impact play?"

She stiffened in his arms.

"I'm going to mark that as a hard limit."

"No." She stilled his hand before he could write. "I want to try flogging."

"Are you sure?"

"Yes." Her beautiful cheeks turned crimson. "I've read about it in the books. They make it sound so sensual."

"It can be." Jordan placed the questionnaire and pen on the side table. "Think of something as soft as a feather caressing your skin." He ran his finger over her forehead and then her nose. "It's soft and sensual." His finger reached her cheek, and he tapped it.

Crystal jumped a little.

"And then I give you a little swat with the flogger." He tapped her cheek again. "Not hard, but not soft. Your nerves wake; your brain tries to process the sensation, and then I do it again." This time, he tapped her chin a little harder. "New and different sensation as the blood flows to the area and your body heats."

She shifted in her seat.

Jordan concentrated on her, taking in her slightly elevated color, the hiccups in her breathing, and how her body relaxed against his. All good signs. "I snap the flogger around your ass, and you squirm with pleasure."

A little moan left her lips. "Oh my," she whispered. "I didn't expect…"

"Expect what?"

"To feel so aroused by your words."

"Thank you for being honest. Words, touches, actions. I will do all I can to arouse you and keep you happy." He brushed his lips over her forehead. "But for now, back to the questionnaire." He reached over and picked up the papers.

"Okay."

"Blindfold?"

"I would call that a soft limit."

"Toys? I mean vibrators, bullets, and clamps."

Crystal shifted against him and laid her hand on his chest. "Those sound okay."

"What about anal play?"

"No." She touched his chin. "If that's okay."

"I'm going to mark it as a hard limit. We can revisit it anytime. These limits aren't set in stone. We can change them at any time."

Her warm breath caressed his skin. "That sounds good."

"Nudity in the club?" Did he want other Doms to see her? He wasn't sure. Interesting he'd never had a problem before with others seeing his play partners. With Crystal, it was different. When she didn't answer, he gazed down at her. Her eyes were closed. "Crystal?"

"I don't know." She swallowed as she shivered. "Can we start off slowly?"

"Sure." He made some quick notes.

"Am I putting too many limits on you?"

"No." It was expected from someone who hadn't experienced the lifestyle before.

"I don't want to disappoint you." Her voice was soft.

"The only way you could disappoint me is by not being honest and communicating with me."

"Thank you." She rubbed her hand over his chest, and his cock tightened.

"Let's finish this up."

"Okay, next." She snuggled closer to him.

Jordan took a deep breath. Concentrate on the questionnaire and not how soft she feels in his embrace or how his cock throbbed with want and need. They had to get this out of the way. Then they could go on to better things.

Pushing his lust aside, Jordan continued. It would take all his control to finish this questionnaire with her, but he'd do it.

They finished up a little while later. Jordan was getting ready to pull Crystal in for a kiss when his phone rang. He lifted his cell from the table and looked at the display.

"I have to take this."

Crystal nodded and removed herself from his embrace. The cool room air hit him.

"Sage, what is it?" He sat forward. "Slow down. What happened?" His mind switched gears quickly.

Crystal shifted in her seat when he said Sage's name.

Jordan listened to Sage, his temper growing. "Sage, take a deep breath. Let me find out what the hell is going on. Next time you get a call like that, tell them to call me." He glanced at Crystal. Her green eyes held concern. "It's okay. Hang in there." He hung up his phone.

"What happened?" Crystal asked softly.

"Brady called Sage. Apparently his family told him there is a new judge, one who will back the family case no matter what is said in court."

"What? That would mean a crooked judge."

"I know." Jordan ran his hand over his short hair. "This was not how I wanted to spend Saturday afternoon with you. But I have to call Brady."

"Do we need to go into the office?"

He noticed the 'we', and some of his tension left his body. "No, I have an office here. I'll call Brady and get the details. Come on, let's get up to speed." Coffee in hand, he led her down the hall to his office. Thank goodness he'd done this years ago. He grabbed one of the extra office chairs and slid it over next to his desk for Crystal, then sat down and turned on his computer.

Within fifteen minutes, he'd talked to Brady, and Crystal was researching what was happening. While they were working, Jordan's cell rang again. He looked at the screen with a frown. "Frost here." Why was the county clerk calling him on a Saturday? Jordan listened, then said, "I want it in email. And the signed order better be in my hands first thing Monday morning." He hung up and closed his eyes.

"Now what?" Crystal asked softly.

"New court date. They've moved the hearing up." He clicked his mouse, and there was the email. With the new court information. "Well, it looks like the judge change is real."

"Bad or good?"

"Not sure." He printed the email and handed it to

her.

"I've dealt with this judge before. I bet he wants to get the lay of the land before this goes any further," Crystal said.

"You're probably right." He sat back in his chair. "We need to get our strategy together."

"We do." She nibbled at her lower lip, and he wanted to kiss away the marks she was making. When she looked up and caught him staring, her cheeks flushed. "I think it would be better if you drove me home."

"Why?" He didn't want her to leave.

"One, because I don't have clean clothes here, and two, someone saw fit to rip my panties this morning." Her cheeks turned a deeper red as she talked.

"Guilty." He wasn't going to apologize for his passion.

"I need to read this document over and so do you. Without distraction."

As much as he wanted to argue with her, she was right. She was a distraction—at least right now. Changing judges at the last minute was a power play by the plaintiffs, which meant he and Crystal needed to revise their original strategy. "How about this? I run you to your apartment; you change and pack an overnight bag and anything else you need, and then we come back here and work."

She tilted her head, which made him want to nuzzle her neck. "Do you think we'll be able to work here?"

"Yes. I can be a good boy." He winked at her, and she laughed. Good, she'd relaxed. He wanted to show her he could control himself.

"Sure you can. Why don't you pick me up

tomorrow morning, and we'll come out here and work. I need to clear my head."

"That sounds ominous." He didn't want to let her go. Logically, he knew he had to let her have her own space.

"Jordan, I haven't been with a man in a while. I need to sort this out by myself." Her voice was strained.

He frowned. "How long has it been?" Why hadn't he thought about asking her before? Maybe because it hadn't mattered to him.

"A few years." Her hand covered his. "I'm not backing away from wanting to be with you; I'm asking for a little space."

Jordan saw the honesty in her eyes. He nodded reluctantly. If anything, he could give her time and space. Not for long, but he'd do it. "Got it." He stood, pulling her with him. "Let's get you home. I'll find a pair of my underwear you can use, unless you want to go commando?"

"Underwear would be nice, thank you."

"Anything for you." He drew her into his arms for a kiss.

Chapter Six

Monday morning, Crystal checked her hair before she left her apartment. Jordan would be here any minute to pick her up. They'd spent all day yesterday going over strategy and… Heat filled her body.

A smile played around her lips as she took the elevator down to the lobby. Jordan had been a gentleman all day. Well, except for those damn hard, passionate kisses he kept giving her.

The second they'd finished preparing for the case, he'd pulled her into his arms and hadn't let her go until early this morning. The things Jordan could do with his hands and mouth. He'd teased and loved her into the early morning hours, driving her home this morning so she could change and get ready for work.

A shudder slid through her body. She enjoyed everything he'd done to her last night, including each and every orgasm he'd given her, and for once, the tapes in her head were silent. Crystal had tried to reciprocate, but he refused, telling her it was all for her. This way she would get used to his touch.

She didn't think she'd ever get used to his touch or the husky tone of his voice when he gave her a command. Crystal bit her lip. She'd more than enjoyed herself last night. Even following his commands didn't dim her need for him.

Jordan pulled up in his dark blue SUV, and she climbed in. His gaze went from the top of her head to the tip of her shoes. "Something wrong?" She'd dressed for court, but opted for pants rather than a skirt, and she'd put her hair up.

"Court Crystal has me all hot and bothered." He leaned over and brushed a kiss against her lips. "Later I'll kiss you silly," he whispered before he pulled away from the curb as she put on her seat belt.

Sage was pacing around the small waiting room when they arrived. "Hi," she said. Crystal noticed the slight tremor in her hands.

"Good morning, Sage." She walked over and hugged the woman. "It will be okay," she whispered.

"Thank you." Sage hugged her back and released her, and Crystal stepped back. "What's our plan of action?" Sage asked Jordan.

"Our first move is to ask for a delay." He held up his hand when Sage opened her mouth. "We're prepared if we need to go forward today, but with the judge change at the last second, we need more time to get some professionals lined up."

Sage nodded. "Okay. I want this to be over with."

"I know you do." Jordan looked at his watch. "Come on. Let's get into that courtroom."

Two hours later, Crystal had a pad full of notes. The judge granted them more time. It had been a fight. Crystal also noticed Brady's family glared at him and kept whispering to the lawyer. Then, whenever Brady tried to say something, the lawyer would object, saying Brady's comments were not relevant to the hearing. Anger welled in her. His family acted like hers did when she was a teenager. She hadn't been allowed to question anything. A shiver slid down her spine. She loved her family, but she would never again put herself in a position that allowed them to control her.

Sage's gaze stayed on Brady as he left the room. "He's lost weight," Sage remarked.

"I noticed," Jordan agreed. He took Sage's arm and escorted her out of the courtroom with Crystal following. After seeing Sage off, they got into Jordan's vehicle.

Jordan took his tie off and tossed it on the seat. "That was not fun."

"No, it wasn't." Her notes were her observations, but still, they were valuable.

"Why don't we stop by Sweet and Savory and have lunch before we go back to the office?"

"I'd like that."

Twenty minutes later, they arrived at Lara's cafe. The place was bustling. "Lara is going to need more help," Crystal said.

"Yeah, I'm glad to see the place so busy." Jordan looked around for a place to sit. There was an empty table next to a group of bikers. He led Crystal over to the table and held out her chair for her. "I'll go order. What would you like?"

She gave him her order, and he got in line. Out of the corner of his eye, he watched Crystal as she talked with the bikers. While some people in the cafe avoided them, Crystal didn't seem to have an issue with them. Good. The bikers he knew were good guys who enjoyed life to the fullest.

Jordan got to the counter, ordered, grabbed their drinks, and returned to the table. The bikers nodded and went back to their food. Crystal turned to him when he sat down.

"Thanks." She opened the water bottle and drank.

"I was thirsty."

"So I see."

"I feel for Sage and Brady."

"I do too. I saw you taking notes; what did you write down?" He'd been surprised to see her scribbling furiously in the notebook as the proceedings went on.

"A lot."

Just then, his name was called, and Jordan retrieved their food and came back. "When you told me you wanted a BCL, I was confused." He set the plate down in front of her.

She laughed. "Bacon, cheese, and lettuce. I hate tomatoes, but Lara knows what I mean."

Crystal picked up her sandwich and took a bite. "Delicious every single time."

Jordan picked up his own ham and cheese and took a bite as Crystal pulled her notebook out of her bag. "Things I wrote about Brady's family. How they were treating him and how they won't let him talk at all. We'll need to get him on the stand to tell his side of the story."

"I noticed the lawyer silencing him. They were like that at the first hearing."

"Something is fishy there." She took another bite of her sandwich and grabbed a napkin when a little bit of mayo dripped on her chin.

"What makes you say that?"

"I observed the dynamic between Brady and his family." She placed the sandwich on the plate and leaned forward. "They remind me of mine." Ice slipped down her spine. She loved her family, but she wouldn't live like they did.

Jordan's warm hand covered hers where it rested on the table. "Tell me." His voice was soft, yet the command was there.

"I told you I grew up in a very strict household. School, homework, chores, that was about it. We weren't allowed to play outside until everything was done to our parents' satisfaction."

"Doesn't sound like fun."

"Nope. I rebelled off and on, but it was like beating my head against a wall. Eventually I stopped when I realized I wasn't going to change and neither were they."

"But you didn't give up on your dreams."

"No." A small smile tilted her lips. "I kept my dreams of a new life in my head." She never wrote any of them down, not after she found her mother reading her sister's diary.

"There's another story there."

"Yes, but not today. Anyway, my parents were religious. We had to go to church every Sunday. The thing I liked was being able to play with the other kids after church and, when I was a teenager, being able to sneak away for a bit."

"I can picture that."

She grinned at him. "I bet you were a terror with your parents."

"Maybe, but we're not talking about me. Go on about Brady's family."

"Well, I saw things that used to happen with my parents. Not allowing us kids to talk. The stern looks and—" She gave a little shake. She couldn't put her finger on it, but there was something in the way Brady's father looked at Sage. Downright hatred.

"And?"

"I know Brady's an adult, but they treat him like

he's a helpless child. I also sense hatred and malice. That's the vibe I'm getting." She glanced over her notes.

"I wouldn't be surprised. What else?"

"Well, I think it would be good if we could talk with someone who knows both Sage and Brady. Someone who has seen them play together, to show this is truly consensual." Jordan frowned, and Crystal pulled her hand from his. "Did I say something wrong?"

"No." He waved his hand in the air. "We can ask. First though, I'd have to make sure Max is on board. But I'll be honest with you, this would likely mean bringing club business into the open."

"Yeah. I don't want to out anyone or the club. I was thinking, if Max was willing, he's probably known them both the longest and can convince the judge of how important consent is in the lifestyle."

Jordan rubbed his hand over his face. "Maybe. I don't want to hang Max and his business out to dry."

"Of course not. That's why this is difficult." She didn't want anyone else to get hurt by this case. "How much does Brady's family actually know?"

"They know about his and Sage's relationship. They don't understand it."

"Do they know about the club?"

"I don't think so. Brady wouldn't have told them."

"All right." She blinked when someone stepped up to the table. Crystal stiffened when she saw a woman holding a cell phone, obviously recording the encounter.

"Mr. Frost, would you care to comment on the case you're working on for Ms. Montgomery?"

"What the—" Jordan clamped his mouth shut.

"Mr. Frost has no comment, and you're disturbing

his lunch. Please leave." Crystal stood and faced the woman reporter.

"And you are?"

"None of your business." Crystal stepped forward, her body language giving the woman the choice to either step back or get pushed. "Out."

"Freedom of the press," the woman said.

"Not in a privately owned business. Once again, Mr. Frost has no comment." Crystal waved her hand toward the door. "You're interfering with the cafe's business." People had stopped and stared, causing a bit of a stir.

"I'm the owner, and I'm asking you to leave now and stop bothering my patrons," Lara said approaching them.

"I have a right to be here." The woman continued.

"The owner has asked you to leave. You are now trespassing. Does she need to call the police?" Crystal kept her tone even. No sense in letting this reporter see she was upset. Which she was. More than upset. There were stringers at the courthouse, and because the judge had denied a motion to seal the record, the case was public. She couldn't see the press being interested since this was listed as a domestic abuse case. Crystal suspected she might know how. Brady's family.

The woman huffed. "You haven't seen the last of me." She turned and stomped out of the cafe.

"Thanks, Lara," Crystal said.

"I swear, some people don't understand personal space." Lara turned and went back to work.

Crystal returned to her seat, her stomach churning. "Now we have a problem." Thank goodness she'd already finished her sandwich. Her stomach was in knots.

"Yes. Stringers are my least favorite people." He gestured out the window to the Channel 5 news truck parked at the curb.

"We need to warn Sage." Should she tell him her suspicions? She didn't have any proof. "I have a feeling Brady's family is behind the reporter."

Jordan swore and pulled his phone out. Crystal put her notebook away and took their empty dishes to the clean-up station. The second they walked outside, the reporter would pounce. They needed another way out.

"Lara," Crystal said. "Can Jordan and I slip out the back to avoid the reporter?" Thank goodness they'd parked in the back lot.

"Sure. Let me know when you're ready."

"Thank you." Crystal went back to the table. Jordan's forehead was lined with worry.

"I told Sage. She's not happy. What a mess."

"Lara told me we can use the back door to leave without the reporter seeing us." She motioned with her head to the news vehicle. Luckily, the occupants couldn't see where she and Jordan were sitting due to the tinted windows.

"Let's go." He took her hand, and they followed Lara out the back.

* * * *

In the following two weeks, they hardly had any time to see each other. The depositions had been completed, and she was busy preparing briefs and doing research, while Jordan was working on his other cases. She was tired, but glad to meet up with Sierra and Tessa for book club night.

"So are you going to tell us about Jordan?" Sierra

said as she drove to the adult store on Wednesday night.

"I'm so curious," Tessa said from the back seat.

"Jordan's a nice guy." Oh yeah, very nice. They hadn't had much alone time since they both had to dodge the reporter every morning and afternoon at the office. Thank goodness, once the woman was escorted from the law office, she didn't come back, but it didn't stop her from being outside every morning and evening.

They were being very careful not to give her anything to speculate about, but Jordan was grouchy.

"Of course, he is," Sierra said.

"Have you slept with him yet?" Tessa asked.

"Tessa." Crystal turned her head in mocking outrage at her friend.

Sierra groaned in sympathy, then asked, "How did you enjoy the club the other week?"

"It's okay." Crystal touched her friend's arm. "It's bound to come out. I'm sorry I haven't had time to catch you two up. Work has been crazy."

"You went to the club? But you're working for Jordan," Tessa said.

"Yes, but the job is short-term, and we have an agreement." Her friends were aware of her mess with dating a lawyer she'd worked with.

"But you went to the club with him?" Tessa asked again.

"I did." She wasn't going to lie to her friend. Sierra already knew because she'd been at the club with Max on Thursday night. "Look, I know I've been busy. But let's have a girls' night on Friday; I have a feeling I'm going to need it." Between the reporter and all the reading she was doing, she needed to give her brain a break.

"I'm game," Tessa said.

"I'll let Max know." Sierra pulled into the parking lot of the store, and they piled out of the car. The monthly book club was something Crystal looked forward to. She'd barely finished the book for this meeting.

They walked in, and Destiny, who ran the store and the book club, waved them to the back. Crystal sighed. She needed to check out the store. If she was going to be Jordan's sub, she needed to get an idea of toys and other stuff.

She looked at her watch; they had twenty minutes before the meeting started. "I'm going to look around," she said, and left her two friends staring after her.

Crystal wandered up and down the aisles, stopping in front of the toy section. There were vibrators, bullets, feathers, dildos, and other items. Her blood heated. She'd never used a toy. She gave a bitter laugh. Her parents would have a heart attack seeing her in this store. What would Jordan think if she brought a toy to the bedroom?

"See anything you like?" A male voice whispered in her ear.

Crystal jerked her head to the left to see Jordan standing there with a grin on his face. "Don't startle me like that." She wanted to be angry with him, but she couldn't. "You didn't mention you'd be here tonight."

"I wasn't sure I would be, but it worked out."

"You are an infuriating man." Tessa's voice carried across the store. Crystal looked over to see her going toe to toe with Damon.

"Oh no," she whispered.

"Damon can handle himself." Jordan cupped her chin and turned her face to him. "Did you find something you'd like to try?"

Crystal ducked her head. Okay, she wasn't a total prude about sex, but this was different for her. Was she ready to share her thoughts with Jordan?

"Sweetheart." Jordan's voice was soft. "It's okay. Am I pushing you?"

"A bit." What was wrong with her? This man had brought her to orgasm with his mouth and his fingers, yet she felt as shy as a girl on her first date. Glancing at the sign on the wall, she smiled. *Embrace your sensuality.* Exactly what she needed to do.

"Crystal." Jordan placed his hands on her shoulders and turned her to him. "I've missed you."

"I've missed you too."

"Ass! Just stay away from me." Tessa's voice broadcasted her exasperation.

"Ummm, Tessa's not happy, and the book club is about to start." While she wanted to talk more with Jordan, now wasn't the time. They needed to be alone for what she wanted to tell him.

"We'll talk later," Jordan slipped his arm around her waist and guided her to the back where they held the book club meetings. Tessa sat in the aisle seat with Sierra and Max next to her, two open seats next to Max, and then Damon.

Tessa's arms were crossed over her chest. Damon looked amused. Crystal and Jordan took their seats as Destiny walked into the room.

"Good evening, everyone. Let's talk about Master Cole."

An hour and half later, the group walked out, talking and joking, except for Damon. He told them he was going to stay behind and look at some items. Tessa snorted and marched out of the store.

Sierra shook her head, and Crystal laughed. Their friend certainly was passionate about not liking Damon. Even so, there was an underlying vibe of attraction from both of them.

"Coffee?" Max asked.

"Not me," Tessa said. "I have an early meeting tomorrow."

"Damn," Crystal whispered. She'd hoped they could talk with Max and Sierra.

"I can run you home and come back," Sierra said.

"I'll take Tessa home," Damon said, stepping outside.

"I'll grab a cab," Tessa countered. "Don't worry about me."

"Like hell you will." Damon put a hand on her shoulder before Tessa could take a step. "Listen. I'll keep my hands and opinions to myself." He lifted his hands in front of him.

Crystal waited. If Tessa said no, she'd back her up.

Tessa nodded. "As long as you keep your word."

"I always keep my word." Damon glanced at them. "She'll be safe with me."

"I believe she will," Sierra said.

Crystal wasn't so sure, but Tessa had agreed.

"Damon will be a complete gentleman." Jordan said.

"I gave my word. I'll drive Tessa home, see her to her door, and then I'll leave. Promise." His words were solemn, but the mischief in his blue eyes made Crystal wonder.

Tessa huffed, turning to Sierra and Crystal.

"Friday night. At Sierra's place?"

"Yes," Sierra piped up.

"Let's go." Tessa started walking to the parking lot, leaving Damon to catch up with her.

"Will they be all right?" Crystal asked.

"They will," Max said. "Damon will escort her home and leave as promised. If not, he knows I'll have his ass."

Sierra laughed. "My hero." She kissed his cheek.

Jordan put his arm around Crystal's waist. "Don't worry. Damon will be on his best behavior." They walked down the street to the coffee shop.

"Jordan mentioned you wanted to speak with me," Max said to Crystal once they were seated with their drinks.

She glanced at Jordan, who nodded. "It's okay."

"It has to do with the Sage and Brady issue." Crystal had been trying to find another way besides Max getting on the stand as a character witness. Nothing had come to light.

"Go on," Max said.

Crystal blew out a breath. This had been her idea. "Look, I don't want to step on any toes or cause any issues, but since you own the club and you've probably known Sage and Brady the longest, I was hoping you'd testify as a character or expert witness."

Max stared at her. "Absolutely." Crystal blinked in astonishment. "But…" Her heart fell. "I already offered, and Sage turned me down."

"When?" Jordan asked.

"When the civil case came to light," Max said.

"She didn't tell me." Jordan took a sip of his coffee. "I need to have a conversation with Sage."

"There has to be a reason," Crystal said. Sage was a bright woman. Why would she turn down Max's offer?

"Sage told me she didn't want to drag me or the club into the court of public opinion."

Movement by the door caught Crystal's attention. "Speaking of which." She jerked her head, and Jordan groaned.

"Fuck."

Before Max or Sierra could say a word. Miss Reporter was in their faces. "Well, this is cozy. Any comments, Mr. Frost?"

Crystal balled her hands in her lap. She so wanted to deck this woman. She was sick of the reporter trying to get information out of them morning and night.

"No comment," Jordan said, draining his coffee cup. Crystal pushed hers away.

"Fine, do you have a comment, Mr. —"

"None of your business." Max's tone was so cold Crystal shivered. He rose to his feet, putting his arm around Sierra as she stood.

Crystal and Jordan followed suit, except Jordan didn't touch her. They'd agreed when the reporter was around, no touching. They walked back to the parking lot with the woman and her cameraman trailing them.

"An adult store. What were you four doing in there?" Her tone was salacious, and Crystal wanted to punch her.

"Seriously?" Sierra said.

"Sierra," Max said.

"For your information the store has a book club. We attended, and that's all there was to it. Now go bother someone else, and leave my friends alone." Sierra's tone was dismissive.

They arrived at Sierra's car. Crystal climbed in, and then Sierra. Max kissed Sierra good night. The men walked to their cars. Crystal could see the indecision about who to follow on the reporter's face.

Sierra took advantage and pulled out of the spot and took off. "That woman is trash," Sierra said.

"I agree. She won't leave us alone."

"About the case?"

"Yes. I'm still trying to find out who told her about it. I have my suspicions." Reporters were always sniffing around the courthouse, but if they found out how groundbreaking this case was…Crystal shook her head.

"Well, you can tell us all about it on Friday."

"Yeah." Crystal laid her head back on the seat. So much for her and Jordan having any alone time together.

* * * *

Crystal finished up with her coffee on Friday morning and started reading through her emails. She'd sent out some feelers into the kink community to see if anyone had come up with anything like the case they were dealing with.

She'd been careful not to say too much so as not to violate Sage and Brady's privacy. After the first three defeats, it hit her. No one had encountered an issue quite like this.

"Well, well, hard at work, are we?"

Crystal glanced up to see Charles Johnson lounging in her doorway. She barely suppressed a sigh. She didn't like this guy at all. "Yes. Are you looking for Valerie or Kendra?" Why else would he be in her office?

"No." He swaggered over to her desk. "I have a—job—that you will take care of."

The predatory gleam in his eye put her senses on

high alert. "Mr. Johnson, I do not work for you."

"You don't." He began to circle her desk. "This has nothing to do with work."

Fuck. She moved quickly so as not to be trapped behind her desk. "Mr. Johnson, I want you to leave." She kept her tone calm even if her nerves quivered with fear. The man had at least fifty pounds on her, but she was quicker.

"I will, but first…" He lunged for her.

Crystal let out a cry and dashed away. But she wasn't quite quick enough.

* * * *

Jordan hung up the phone for the fifth time in thirty minutes and sat back in his chair. Damn reporter. He stared at the newspaper article, or more precise, gossip column. The reporter talked about how he and Crystal were spotted at the local adult store for book club night with friends.

Luckily, she hadn't mentioned the case or identified Max or Sierra. But people had seen the article and called him. He needed to warn Crystal. He stood and headed for her office.

He heard Crystal cry out and raced the last few feet, his heart thudding. Inside, he froze at the sight in front of him.

Crystal's hair was mussed, as well as her blouse. Johnson had her by the arm, and Crystal struggled in his hold. Her eyes were wide, but her lips were pressed together in a thin line.

Johnson, on the other hand, was huffing and puffing, his shirt half pulled out of his pants. He pushed Crystal toward her desk, her arm flew out, and papers flew from her desk. Johnson was right behind her with his hand on her hip.

Jordan's fists clenched. "Let her the fuck go." Within three strides, he was on Johnson, pulling him away and throwing him up against the wall. Anger filled his veins.

"Why should I? According to that nice little newspaper article, you're getting some, so why shouldn't I?" Johnson sneered.

Jordan's arm came up and pinned the man by the neck, cutting off his airflow. "Bastard." He pushed harder. This man was trash, and it was time he threw the garbage out. He should have done that to his father before he killed his mother.

"Jordan." Crystal's soft voice brought his attention to her. "It's okay." She placed her hand on his arm. "Please, let him go. He's not worth it."

Jordan turned to Crystal. Her gaze was on him, not Johnson. Those beautiful green eyes shone with trust and care.

The dark anger receded, and he released Johnson, who wheezed in a few sharp breaths.

"Johnson, you are fired."

"You can't fire me," he wheezed out.

Jordan turned his head and glared at him. "This is my firm, and I certainly can fire your ass. Get out. I'll make sure someone sends you your personal items."

"Come on, Jordan. You're going to fire me over a piece of ass?"

Crystal groaned. "You don't know when to shut up, do you?" she muttered.

"Apparently, he doesn't." Jordan forced himself to breathe in and out in an effort to keep his temper under control. He wanted nothing more than to throttle Johnson.

"Crystal, do you want to press the appropriate charges?"

She raised her chin. "Here's the deal. Mr. Johnson, you leave and keep your mouth shut, and I won't press charges. But you so much as breathe a single word about me, Jordan, or the firm, and I'll will see you're prosecuted to the fullest extent of the law and sue you in civil court." Crystal's voice was firm, and Jordan was proud of her for standing up to the man. His woman was no pushover.

When Johnson didn't answer, Jordan said, "Call security," he told Crystal.

"All right, I'll leave."

Jordan took a step back but made sure Crystal was behind him. He kept his eye on Johnson as the man straightened his shirt.

"I'll be taking my clients with me."

"Let me call security so I can press charges." Crystal reached for her phone.

"Fine. I'll keep my mouth shut." Johnson started to the door.

Jordan followed the man. "Be right back," he said over his shoulder to Crystal as he kept on Johnson's ass. He was going to make sure he left.

* * * *

After straightening her clothes and quickly finger-combing her hair, Crystal fell onto her office chair and put her head in her hands. How had things gotten out of control so fast? One minute Johnson was across the room from her, the next, he had her by the arm and was trying to kiss her and more. A shudder racked her body.

She'd been about to scream her head off, and suddenly, Jordan arrived. How did he always seem to know when she needed him? Crystal took care of herself.

Always had. But the sense of security from knowing he was there for her softened every edge of her angst. And the look on Jordan's face? Pure, unadulterated anger at someone who dared to hurt her. Her. No one had ever cared about her like that before.

"Crystal, are you okay?" Jordan asked quietly as he re-entered her office.

"I am." She kept her gaze on him as he slipped onto the chair in front of her desk. His face was still a bit flushed from his anger, but there was concern there as well. Concern for her. "Are you okay?"

He laughed. "Yeah. I'm sorry that happened. Has Johnson tried anything before?"

"No, and I don't know what made him think he could today." It didn't make sense.

"I might have some insight into that, but first, I want to apologize for my temper."

"Temper? I would say you controlled it very well."

"I was about to deck him when you put your hand on my arm."

"Yeah, well, I should've let you, but I didn't want him to press assault charges against you, even though he deserved it. So what did you find out?" She was actually glad she could help Jordan clear his head.

"The reporter has put out a story on us."

Crystal closed her eyes and opened them. "How bad?"

"It reads more like a gossip column. Basically tells about us being at the adult store on Wednesday night."

"Give me the website."

"Check your email." He'd sent her the link. She

clicked her mouse and then started at her screen. "Innuendo and speculation." She blew out a breath.

"Yes."

"Did you talk with Sage?" she asked.

"I did." Unproductive call. "She won't have Max or the club dragged into this. Even though that's the only place she and Brady play."

"They don't play at home?"

"According to Sage, no. She said their sexual relationship has been kept to the club, although I suspect they might have been ready to go to the next level when this all started."

"Yeah." Crystal rubbed her forehead.

"Headache?" Jordan stood and walked behind her.

"A bit. I've been reading these dry law books all day."

He placed his hands on her shoulders and started to massage. Oh yeah, she was tight. He worked the knots out.

"Oh that feels so good."

"Why don't we go to my place tonight? I can give you a good massage."

Crystal's head dropped forward, giving him more room to massage her neck. "I'd love to, but it's girls' night at Sierra's. I can't miss it."

"I'd forgotten." Maybe he'd go to the club and help Max out. He wasn't officially on duty until tomorrow night. They tried to split up the duties between the three of them and occasionally, a couple of the trusted Doms.

Max rarely took time off, and Jordan was trying to get him to take more since he had Sierra.

"Maybe tomorrow night." Her voice was hopeful.

"I'm working at the club tomorrow night, but you could always come with me."

"Now that sounds fun." She shifted in her seat.

"A date then." He leaned down and brushed a kiss over her cheek before straightening. "How about I pick you up at five? We can grab dinner and then go to the club."

She leaned her head back and frowned at him. "Dinner? But what about how we're dressed?"

"Put your club clothes in a bag; you can change once we get to the club."

"I forgot about the changing area." She shrugged her shoulders. "Go. I've got to finish this reading before I leave."

"Bossy," he said with a laugh.

"Anytime you want to bottom, let me know." She clamped her hand over her mouth. Where had those sassy words come from?

Jordan wagged a finger at her. "Ms. Hayden, you are being naughty." He leaned over. "Tomorrow night, I might punish you for your naughtiness." He straightened and left the office with a big smile on his face.

* * * *

"Okay, we've eaten. Spill." Tessa demanded.

Dinner had been from their favorite pizza place, and now Crystal was curled up in the overstuffed chair while Sierra and Tessa were on the sofa.

"Yeah, spill. I need details," Sierra said.

"Yeah," Tessa waved her hand. "You went to the club with him?"

"I did. I know this will not go out of this room. I went because it had to do with the case I am working on with him, and that's all I'm going to say."

Tessa's eyes widened, and Sierra nodded.

"I enjoyed going to the club and being able to talk with people in the lifestyle." Crystal looked at Sierra. "I know you're there a lot now, but you never mentioned the other people."

"Part of the NDA. We can't discuss specific people, but we can discuss what happened. Like the scene Jordan helped with."

"Oh yeah." Crystal squirmed in her seat as she remembered the deep timbre of Jordan's voice and the way it seemed to caress her skin.

"She's squirming. There's something to tell there," Tessa said, clapping her hands.

"Why are you so interested in my love life?" Crystal asked.

"Hey, I live vicariously between you and Sierra and the books I read," Tessa said.

"You know Damon would take you out and fulfill your fantasies," Sierra said.

"Please." Tessa rolled her eyes. "His views on women are old school. I don't want a man to tell me what to do. I want to be a partner in life. So you and Jordan, have you slept together yet?"

"Yes, and no." Crystal shook her head. Tessa was protesting too much. There was definitely something between her and Damon.

"That's not an answer," Sierra said.

"Well, I had dinner at his house Friday night almost two weeks ago. We ate and talked, and I fell asleep. When I woke the next morning, I was in bed with him."

"He didn't take advantage, did he?" Sierra frowned.

"No." Her cheeks warmed. "He did undress me, but he was a gentleman. Well, until he kissed me." Her body heated, remembering that morning. "Let's say the interlude we had would have knocked my socks off if I'd been wearing any."

"So you did have sex with him?" Tessa asked.

"Ummm…no." Why was this so hard to get out? These were her friends. "Jordan went down on me, and I climaxed."

The two women squealed, and Crystal ducked her head. She'd never learned the basics of sex. Her old boyfriends never went down on her; they were more about wanting to order a woman around and make her a sexual toy.

"Hey," Sierra said, "don't be embarrassed."

"It's hard." Crystal took a breath. "I was raised in a strict family where sex wasn't talked about." She'd given them the basics about her family but not much. She didn't like talking about them.

"Us girls talk about it," Sierra said.

"And read," Tessa added.

"We do." There was nothing wrong with it. She enjoyed what Jordan did to her. Enough of being a coward. "Okay, then the weekend before last, Jordan teased me with his hands and lips until I was going crazy. I climaxed, but that's as far as he'd let it go." She waved her hand. "With everything going on, we've not had much alone time."

"Oh man, Jordan sounds like he enjoys teasing you," Sierra said.

"He does." Crystal ducked her head. "I agreed to become his sub." The room went silent.

"That's wonderful," Sierra said.

"Are you sure? You said yourself you're not used to talking about sex, and the lifestyle requires a lot of communication between parties."

Sierra's eyes widened, and Crystal stared at Tessa. "How do you know so much?" Sierra asked.

Tessa bit her lip and looked down. "I told you—reading and through you two."

"Hmmm." Sierra tapped her foot.

Crystal decided to rescue Tessa. "It does take a lot of communication. I'm learning, and Jordan understands. I've told him about my family."

"And how did he react?" Sierra turned her attention back to Crystal.

"As I said, he understands. We both agreed we'd make mistakes." Crystal took a drink. "There is another thing."

"This doesn't sound good," Tessa said.

"It's not." She blew out a breath. "Earlier today, one of the other lawyers in the office sexually assaulted me."

"What the fuck?" Sierra jumped to her feet.

"I hope you sue his ass," Tessa said. She reached over and grasped Crystal's hand.

"Sierra, sit down please." Crystal squeezed Tessa's hand. "Here's the thing. The reporter who followed us the other night wrote up an article. It's nothing but speculation and innuendo. But this seemed to empower Johnson to come after me." A tremor shook her body.

"Bastard." Sierra's arm went around her shoulder. "I'll tell Max. He'll make the man pay."

"No." Crystal's voice was firm. "Jordan took care of Johnson according to my wishes."

"Which were?" Tessa asked.

"Well, Jordan fired him first, then Johnson threatened to take his clients."

"I bet Jordan didn't react well to that," Tessa said.

"No, but basically, I told Johnson if he breathes anything about me, Jordan, or the firm, or tries to take his clients, I'll press charges in criminal court and then sue him in civil court."

"Do you think he'll keep quiet?" Sierra asked.

"He better. Can you imagine what Max and Jordan will do to him?"

"Damon too," Tessa piped up and then ducked her head as she released Crystal's hand. "He seems like that type of man."

Interesting, Crystal thought. Maybe Tessa was more interested in Damon than she let on. She'd need to watch those two when they were together.

"He is," Sierra said. "They all are."

"I'm sure. Anyway, I'm going back to the club with Jordan tomorrow night."

"Isn't Jordan on duty?" Sierra asked.

"He is, but I want to observe more. There are still a lot of things that don't match with the books we read." Not much but it was there.

"I'm going to live vicariously through you two," Tessa said.

Crystal frowned at her friend. "I thought you had a date earlier this week?" Had she missed a change in Tessa's life?

"It was one date, and he never called afterward."

"Ass," Sierra commented. "I can ask Max if he'll allow you to come to the club on a Thursday night. Those are usually pretty quiet nights, and you could see what goes on."

Tessa shook her head and pressed her hand against her belly. "I'd rather not."

Crystal opened her mouth, but Sierra motioned to her. Crystal nodded.

"Well, if you change your mind, let me know. So do we want to watch a movie or what?"

"Movie." Tessa piped up. "Something different."

Crystal wondered what was going through Tessa's head. She wanted to ask, but Tessa would talk when she was ready.

"Different." Sierra started flipping through her DVDs.

Crystal grinned. Sierra wouldn't get rid of her prized DVD collection no matter what. "Something other than what we usually watch, I'm guessing?" Sierra commented.

"Yes. No rom-coms or romance tonight. I need something different," Tessa said.

"Hmmm." Sierra kept flipping, then she pulled out a DVD with a smile. "What about *300*."

Tessa's face lit up, and Crystal laughed. "I think we have a winner."

Chapter Seven

Wicked Sanctuary was busy on Saturday night. More club members and noise. Jordan had been busy since they stepped inside the doors.

Crystal had dressed a little more daring tonight. Her skirt fell below her knees, and she wore a lace shawl over her corset. She didn't mind that Jordan was working. When she arrived, he'd escorted her to what he called the green area and told her to stay there and watch. If a Dom approached, she should hold up her arm. Her wristband would show them she was taken.

"I see you didn't run away," a female voice said.

Crystal glanced up to see Sage walking up in leather pants, high-heeled boots, and a black corset. "How the hell do you walk in those things?" Crystal blurted out, noticing the four-inch spiked heels. "Sorry, Mistress Sage." Protocol inside the club.

"Very carefully." Sage smiled and sat down next to Crystal. "And it's Sage. Jordan on duty tonight?"

"Yes. I wanted to observe the club some more." She was glad to have someone to talk to.

"Good night for it, and I'm glad I'm here." Sage glared over Crystal's shoulder.

Crystal started to turn.

"No, Crystal." Sage tapped Crystal's chin. "Keep your eyes on me, please."

She was startled by Sage's words but didn't say a thing.

Sage chuckled. "No worries. There was a Dom eyeing you, and I didn't want Jordan to rush over here."

"Oh, but…" She lifted her arm to show Sage her wristband. "Jordan said this would show I was taken."

"It would. Let's say I didn't want the Dom to step into our arena right now."

Crystal tilted her head. There was something Sage wasn't telling her. Maybe she'd find out later.

"Ah Sage, good to see you," Jordan said, leaning down and kissing her cheek. "Are you playing tonight?"

"No. I needed to get out of my apartment and my head."

Jordan nodded. "Would you mind staying with Crystal? She wants to watch the action and might need some explanations."

"I sure can." Sage smiled.

"Thank you." Jordan moved to her and leaned down. "Ask Sage any questions you have. Enjoy." He took her lips in a hard, fast kiss and was off.

Crystal sighed as she watched him walk away. Damn, the man could kiss, and he also had one fantastic backside.

"Come on, Cinderella, let's continue your education."

* * * *

Jordan bundled Crystal into his SUV at two in the morning. Damon volunteered to close, and Jordan took him up on the offer. There were a few diehards left in the club.

Crystal was out on her feet. Jordan draped a blanket he kept in his vehicle over her before he slipped her seatbelt on. Once he pulled out, it took a few minutes for the car to warm up, and he turned on the heater.

"That feels good," she said softly.

"Let me know if you get too hot." It was almost the end of January, and while it was cool, the weather didn't bother him, but Crystal had complained when they walked out of the club.

He drove home quickly, occasionally glancing over at her. Her eyes were closed, and her breathing deep and even. He probably should have warned her it was going to be a long night.

Jordan yawned. He was used to having long nights on Friday and Saturday. He used Sunday as a catch up day. He pulled into his garage and smiled. Catching up with Crystal tomorrow would be fun.

After taking off her seatbelt, he pulled her into his arms and made his way into his house. She snuggled up to him. He couldn't help thinking of the first time he'd put her in his bed.

With a grin playing around his lips, he took off her club clothes. Thank goodness she'd told him about the hidden zipper in her corset. He tucked her into bed and frowned when he noticed the bruise on her shoulder. He could see the faint outline of fingers. Johnson. He'd grabbed her by the shoulder. Jordan's anger boiled up and threatened to spill out. There was only one way he was going to get to sleep tonight.

Straightening, he padded out of the room and down the hallway to his home gym. If one could call it a gym. There wasn't much in it. A small dresser, punching bag, and a chair. Walking over to the dresser, he pulled out a pair of shorts and changed, then he wrapped his hands. He needed to let off some steam before he climbed into bed with Crystal.

Thirty minutes later, Jordan swept the sweat out

of his eyes, took a swig of water from the bottle he had on the dresser, and went back to the bag. He pictured Johnson's face each time he hit the bag.

He reflected back on high school when some boys were picking on another boy. Jordan had become so enraged he took four boys on. When he calmed down, the four boys were on the ground, and several teachers were staring at him. Luckily, no one was hurt, but it could have been worse.

Maybe Jordan was more like his father than he thought.

* * * *

Crystal turned onto her back and opened her eyes. Where was she? The last thing she remembered was being in Jordan's vehicle and… She fell asleep. She glanced at her shoulder and frowned. When did she get a bruise? The memory of Johnson grabbing her filtered through her brain. Damn. Jordan wouldn't have missed the bruise when he undressed her.

She turned again. The other side of the bed was empty. She glanced at the clock on the side table. Five. Maybe he was in the kitchen getting a snack. Lord, she hoped so. Standing, she shivered as cool air caressed her skin. She only had panties on. Grabbing her shawl from where it was draped on the chair, she threw it over her shoulders and went to find Jordan.

She crept toward the kitchen, but the lights were off. She turned. There were lights on down the hall, and she could hear faint repeated thuds. Curious, she made her way in the direction of the light.

The noise got louder as she approached the room. The door was half open. Not wanting to disturb Jordan, she peeked inside the room, and her breath locked in her throat.

Jordan was hitting a punching bag, and judging by the amount of sweat running down his body, he'd been doing it for a while. His muscles bunched as he punched right then left.

"Take that, Johnson," he muttered.

The power behind his punches made the bag sway. Crystal wanted to go to Jordan and tell him she was fine, but she also understood his need to work out what he was feeling. He wasn't a man to keep things bottled up.

She stood silently and watched until he stopped.

"Fuck," he muttered, and dropped his head forward as if defeated.

Crystal's heart pounded. She longed to go to him, but something told her this proud man wouldn't want her to see him this way.

When he raised his head, she quietly backed away and padded back to the bedroom. They both had demons they needed to deal with. His temper and her family.

* * * *

Jordan unwrapped the tape from his hands. He grimaced when he flexed them. He'd gone at it too long and hard, but he needed to work out his anger. Back in the bedroom, he glanced at the bed. Good. Crystal was still asleep.

It was almost five-thirty. He needed some sleep, but first, a shower. He was sweaty.

He cleaned up, thinking about the night. Even though he'd been busy with his DM duties, he'd kept an eye on Crystal while she was with Sage. They'd taken in a bondage scene, a flogging scene, and a punishment scene.

There had been times when he wanted to go to Crystal, pull her into his arms, and hold her. Especially during the punishment scene. She'd been obviously uncomfortable and kept looking away or looking at Sage.

At one point, he was sure Sage asked her if she wanted to leave, but Crystal shook her head. He wondered why. There was no reason to stay at a scene if it wasn't your thing. He'd have to make sure she understood she had the right not to watch a scene.

Clean and dry, he sauntered back into his bedroom. Crystal was curled up, still asleep. Jordan climbed into bed with her and pulled her into his arms.

She snuggled right up to him, and he was sure he was the luckiest man alive. A few hours sleep, and then he'd wake her in the most delicious way.

* * * *

Jordan shifted in his sleep. Such a nice dream, Crystal was kissing her way over his chest and his abs to his groin. Her hand encircled his dick. Her skin was cool against his overheated body.

She stroked him, once, twice. Oh yeah. He groaned. Damn, he wanted more than her hand, but his dreams never went further for some reason. Wait a second…a tongue swept over the head of his cock.

"Crystal, baby," he murmured.

Warm breath wafted over his erection. Too real. A warm mouth enveloped his dick. His eyes opened.

"Fuck," he said. He hadn't been dreaming. Crystal had his shaft in her mouth. Their gazes locked.

She lifted her head. "Good morning," she said before lowering her mouth over him once again.

"Honey," he said. "You don't have to do this." Hell, he always woke with a morning erection, but it didn't mean she had to do anything about it.

She didn't answer. Instead, her fingers encircled his base as she drew him farther into her mouth. Her tongue danced and licked his cock.

A groan left his lips as his body reacted. Up and down she went, using her mouth and hand. His erection grew. She lifted her mouth and licked him root to tip.

Damn. His breath caught in his throat. The feel of her tongue on his shaft sent shockwaves through his veins.

"So hard. So much mine." Her voice was soft, but the gleam in her eyes caused his groin to tighten.

When she took him in her mouth, she sucked and stroked his dick in time with her hand. His balls quivered. He wasn't going to last. "Baby, I'm going to come." The women he'd dated over the years didn't like swallowing, and he'd only played this way with one sub who'd liked it when he came all over her breasts.

Crystal didn't stop, but started stroking and sucking him harder. His toes flexed, and he clenched his hands into fists so as not to reach for her. The last thing he wanted to do was scare her by grabbing her head and holding her down. "Crystal," he moaned. Then his cock twitched.

He came in spurts, and she lapped every drop down. She even licked him clean before she removed her mouth from his dick. She glanced at him from beneath her lashes with a cat-like grin on her lips.

Jordan sat up, pulled her to him, and covered her lips. His salty essence touched his taste buds as he toyed with her tongue.

"I guess you liked it," she said, breaking the kiss and breathing heavy.

"I loved it. Not many women swallow."

"I wanted to see how you tasted." Her cheeks turned pink.

"It's a nice way to wake up." He leaned back, pulling her onto his chest.

"Well, I thought it fair since you did it for me the last time."

"It wasn't necessary." This woman could surprise him.

"I know, but I wanted to." Her cheeks turned darker.

She was hiding something. And then it dawned on to him. "You saw this happen in the club last night?" Crystal ducked her head, and he knew he'd scored. "Aw, sweetheart." He put his fingers beneath her chin and raised her head up. "Nothing to be embarrassed about."

"I can't help it." She kept her lashes lowered. "There are times I still hear my parents saying sex is a sin."

No wonder she'd been so conflicted about things. "There is nothing wrong with sex or enjoying it. Your parents had sex to have you and your brothers and sisters."

"According to my mom, you endure for procreation."

Jordan wanted to smack both her parents. "Sex for pleasure is not a sin." He ran his fingers over her cheek. "What you did for me was wonderful."

She shook her head.

"Then what is it? Because there is something else."

When she didn't say anything, Jordan moved. He rolled her onto her back with him over her so he could see her face better. Color was still high in her cheeks. Her nipples rubbed against his chest, and her legs entwined with his. All good signs.

"Look at me, Crystal." He kept his tone low and even. "Now." She raised her lashes at the command behind the word. Her eyes were wary. "Now tell me what has you so worried?" He needed and wanted to know so he could help her.

She cleared her throat. "I was told I was unresponsive in bed."

Jordan blinked several times, not believing the words she'd spoken. There was no way he could do this lying on top of her. He rolled to his side and sat up. A soft sigh floated in the air.

"You…" He turned and maneuvered her body around his until she was sitting in his lap. "…are very responsive." He placed his palm on her cheek. "The asshole who told you that knows nothing about women."

"But—"

He placed his fingers against her lips. "No. He's wrong. One hundred percent wrong." Her green eyes widened at his declaration. "You are responsive to the right man. Me." Her lips curved up, and he removed his fingers.

"You mean that?"

"Yes. Lord, yes. Don't you know that? Besides, not all men can arouse a woman."

"So I'm not a cold, unfeeling bitch?"

Jordan's temper flared, but he tamped it down. No more anger. He wasn't his father, and he wasn't mad at her, but he was angry at the ass who'd made her doubt herself as a woman. "No." He ran his fingers over her naked back, and she shivered. "That tremor there. It was one of arousal."

"How do you know?"

"You leaned into my touch, didn't pull away."

"I guess I never thought about it."

"So don't let anyone feed you that kind of bullshit." He shifted. "I have a question for you."

"Yes?" She stared into his handsome face.

"How do you feel about playing at the club?"

"Depends."

"On what?" His fingers caressed her naked back.

"On what you want to do and how undressed I would be." She'd been thinking about this. "I don't want to be naked."

"I agree; I don't want you naked." His palm splayed against her skin. "Are you open to negotiating what will happen at the club the night we play?"

She tilted her head. "Yes." A tingle slid over her spine in anticipation of what their club play would be like.

"Since that's out of the way." He flipped her onto her back on the bed. "I believe it's my turn."

"Your turn?"

"Yep." He leaned over and took her hard nipple in his mouth, sucked and licked it before raising his head. "So aroused for me."

"Jordan," she said.

"We're in the bedroom, sweetheart."

"Oh, yes…Sir."

His cock twitched at the 'sir'. Jordan shifted until he had her body in the middle of his bed. "Arms over your head."

She complied, and he kissed her softly before opening the side table drawer. He drew out some light cuffs and tossed them on the bed. Her eyes grew wide.

"You keep restraints next to your bed, Sir?"

"Among other things. Are you okay with them?"

"Yes, Sir."

He slipped the first restraint on her wrist and then the second one. Then he tested the tightness. "Feel okay?" he asked.

"It's fine, Sir."

He nodded, then took a length of rope out of the drawer. He drew the rope through the D rings on the cuffs then through the ring on the headboard and tied it off. Jordan took a pair of scissors out of the drawer.

"Why scissors, Sir?"

"They're in case I need to release you quickly." He rummaged in the drawer and pushed the blindfold away. *Too soon.* His fingers closed over plastic packaging and pulled it out.

Crystal squirmed, and her eyes widened when she saw what he was holding. He was on the right track. Jordan tore open the packaging and pulled out the toy. "Be right back." He stood. He wasn't going far. Rule number one in bondage: Never leave someone bound and alone.

The bathroom had a direct line of sight to the bed, and he left the door open as he washed the toy quickly and grabbed a towel.

Crystal's gaze stayed with him the whole time. Her body was flushed, and she couldn't stop wiggling on the bed.

"Have you ever used a vibrator?" he asked, pulling a condom out of the drawer.

"No, Sir," she whispered.

He stopped and looked at her. "You have brought

yourself off before, haven't you?"

Her face turned red. "Yes, Sir." Her voice was soft.

Jordan sighed with relief. While he'd brought her to climax last week using his mouth, her not using a toy had surprised him. "With your fingers?"

She nodded.

"Well, this is going to be a little bit different." He slipped the condom on the toy and knelt between her legs. With a gentle touch, he ran his finger over her mound. She shifted and spread her legs wider.

Jordan slipped a finger between her pussy lips. Moisture greeted him. "So what else did you see at the club last night?" he asked as he fingered her pussy.

"The club, Sir?" Her words were heavy with her breathing.

"What did you and Sage watch besides the fellatio scene?" He continued to finger her, arousing her body for the toy.

"Umm, a bondage scene, Sir."

"Ah yes. You need to see Max do a bondage scene with Sierra. Max is a master at it."

"Max and Sierra, Sir?"

He glanced up at her. Her eyes were a little wide. "Did I embarrass you with that tidbit?"

"No, but I never thought about watching Max and Sierra in a scene, Sir."

"There are lots of people at the club who are friends outside the club as well. It's nothing to worry about." He slipped his finger from her pussy. She was ready. He placed the head of the vibrator at her entrance and slid it in.

"Ohhh." Her hips rose.

"Like that?" He twisted the toy and pushed it farther into her body.

"It's different. Hard, not as warm, Sir."

"It will be warm soon enough." He gently moved the vibrator in and out of her pussy. "What else did you watch?"

"A flogging scene, Sir."

Interesting. "Mild or heavy?"

"I'm not sure I know what you mean, Sir."

"What kind of implement did the Dom use?"

"I don't know, Sir."

"I see I need to educate you more." He turned the vibrator on.

"Oh." Her body jerked.

Sweet, sweet, Crystal. He'd barely started, and her pussy walls were already tightening around the toy, making it hard for him to move it. "What are you feeling?"

"Feeling, Sir?" Her voice was a bit breathless.

"Yes, feeling. Does the toy make you tingle? Are you scared?" He continued to stroke her with the toy.

"Tingles and… I don't know. It feels different, maybe because of the vibrations." She shifted on the mattress. "I've never felt anything like it, Sir."

He wasn't surprised. From what little bit she'd told him, her upbringing would have made her hesitant about too much self-pleasure. "How are your arms doing?"

"They're fine, Sir."

Jordan tilted his head and stared at Crystal. She was telling the truth. Good. He continued to tease her with the vibrator until she continuously squirmed on the bed. His dick throbbed.

He pulled the toy from her wet pussy and set it on the nightstand where he'd placed the towel. Crystal's gaze was on him when he pulled fresh condom out and sheathed himself.

Her intake of breath caused him to pause. "Baby, are you okay with this?" While they'd talked, and there was consent between them, her swift intake of breath told him something wasn't quite right.

"Please, Sir." She wiggled her hips. "I want you. I need you, Sir."

Jordan carefully lowered himself over her. His heart pounded as his cock brushed her entrance, and the heat coming from her singed his skin. She was ready for him.

"More, Sir."

Shifting his hips, Jordan pushed into her willing pussy. Inch by inch, he sank into her until he was fully seated.

"Damn, you're a big guy, Sir." Her face was flushed, her eyes a little unfocused.

"I bet you say that all the time," he teased. Her face turned a darker shade of red. She opened her mouth to reply, but he shifted, and she moaned instead. "I'm teasing you. How are your arms?"

"My arms, Sir?"

"Are they numb? Do they hurt?" He started to withdraw from her body.

Her legs encircled his waist. "I'm fine, Sir."

He stared down at her. "Flex your fingers." She did. No distress on her face, but still… Her legs tightened when he shifted.

"Truly, I'm okay, Sir. Hands and arms are fine, Sir."

Her words were clear and filled with need, not pain or discomfort. "All right, my sweet." He slid back into her slick pussy. "Here we go." Jordan surged into her.

Crystal moaned, her neck arching as Jordan plunged into her pussy. Oh dear Lord, his cock was hard and pulsing. But he didn't rush; he took his time, out and in.

* * * *

Her body was on fire. Her clit throbbed with need. She clenched her fingers and released them. There was a slight tingle in her arms, but she wasn't going to stop Jordan. She wanted this. She wanted him.

"Harder, faster," she whispered.

"What was that?" His breath brushed over her skin like a silky caress.

She opened her eyes to see him staring down at her, his body still. "Sir, please." Damn! She needed to remember he was in charge.

"Better." His voice was calm, but he didn't speed up, and her body protested. She was right on the edge. It wouldn't take much to throw her over. Crystal tightened her legs around him.

"Sweetheart, you're trying to top from the bottom." There was amusement in his voice, but she had no idea what he meant. "Loosen your legs, or I'll stop."

"You wouldn't dare."

His body stilled.

Fuck. Where did he get his iron control? Crystal forced her legs to go lax around his waist.

"Better but do it again, and I will stop."

"Yes, Sir." She tried to sound contrite but wasn't sure she pulled it off.

Jordan began thrusting once again, and she raised her hips. While he didn't say anything, the way he stared at her, he was aware of what she was doing. Finally, he moved faster, their hips grinding together.

Her body quivered on the precipice, the right thrust or touch and… Jordan shifted his hips and hit her g-spot. Crystal let out a little cry as her orgasm took over.

He didn't stop moving until he stiffened, and his cock pulsed inside her as he came. He collapsed against her body, but he didn't crush her.

"Damn, you are so sweet." His lips met hers in a languid kiss. When he lifted his head, his eyes were a bit unfocused.

"I hate to ruin this, but my fingers are tingling. Though it could be from the orgasm you gave me."

"You do have the expression of a well-fucked, very satisfied woman."

Her cheeks flamed as she rose up and nipped his lips.

"Witch." Jordan rose. He released the restraints and massaged her arms. "Better?" She nodded. "Good. Be right back." He went into the bathroom and disposed of the condom and returned.

Jordan laid down next to her and pulled her into his arms. "You are special," he whispered.

"I think you're the special one."

Their lips met in a soft, afterglow type of kiss. Crystal parted her lips and nipped at his mouth. Jordan pulled back and stared down at her. "I want to play some more."

"Let's."

The tone of his cell phone cruelly and abruptly interrupted their plans. Jordan groaned but ignored it. He played with Crystal's nipples, watching them harden. His phone went off again, and he ignored it. By the third time, he realized it had to be important.

With a groan, he sat up and reached for the device. "Frost here."

"Oh God, Jordan. I need you."

"Sage?" He could barely understand her through her tears.

"It's a mess."

"What's a mess?" Jordan cradled his phone as he sat up.

"Everything."

"Where are you?"

"At home. Get here as fast as you can. I can't do this anymore."

The line went dead, and Jordan swore. He turned to Crystal. "That was Sage, something's happened."

"Do you know what?" She was already moving to stand.

"No. She just said she can't do this anymore." Jordan ran his hand over his face. "What the hell could be going on?"

"Let's get dressed and go find out." Crystal was already halfway across the room to the bag she'd packed for last night.

"Agreed, but—" Jordan hesitated.

"What is it?" Crystal moved to his side.

"What if she's suicidal? Shouldn't I call emergency services?"

Crystal tilted her head. "Sage doesn't strike me as someone who would take her life. We talked a lot last night. I think she's tired of this trial and being apart from Brady."

"True, but I'm worried."

Crystal walked over and put her arms around him, hugging him. "Then let's get moving. The sooner we get out of here, the sooner we can find out what is going on with Sage."

"You're right." He squeezed her close for a minute, then released her. "Go clean up, I'll use the guest bath."

"I'm willing to share."

Jordan stared at her.

"Nothing more than getting cleaned up and getting to Sage. So wipe that look off your face." She grinned at him.

His heart lightened. Crystal was good for him.

* * * *

Forty-five minutes later, Jordan was knocking on Sage's front door. Pounding was more like it. Crystal understood. He was worried. She put her hand on his tense arm as the door opened.

"Thank goodness," Sage said. "Get in here."

They stepped inside her house. Sage's face was tear-stained, her voice a bit wobbly.

"What's happened?" Jordan asked.

Crystal's gaze snapped to the person sitting on the sofa, huddled under a blanket. "Brady," she said softly.

Jordan swore. "Sage, I thought you two agreed to keep your distance while this case was going on."

"Fuck that," Sage bit out.

Crystal ignored them and walked over to Brady. "Hi Brady, I'm Crystal. I'm not sure if you remember me from court."

"I do." Brady was a good-sized man, but she could see his hands were trembling. Something was off here.

"What can we do to help you?" she asked softly. Asking if he was okay wasn't an option. It was obvious he wasn't okay. Lord, how many times had she seen this with her own family. The absolute fear. Her heart clenched along with her stomach.

"They're going to kill me," he whispered as his gaze went to where Sage and Jordan stood arguing.

"Who Brady?" Her nerves twitched.

"My family." His eyes were huge. "I thought they'd come around. Damn it, I'm an adult, a physician, old enough to have my own life." His tone emphasized the depth of his anger.

Not good. There was something very wrong here. "I'll be right back." Crystal strode over to Sage and Jordan. "Sage, is there another room I can take Brady into while you two hash this out?"

Sage's gaze went to Brady, then back to her. The concern and worry in those brown eyes warmed Crystal's heart.

"There's a guest bedroom down the hall and to the left. It has its own bathroom," Sage said.

"He shouldn't stay," Jordan said.

Crystal looked Jordan straight in the eye. "This isn't about the damn case; it's about Brady." If he didn't understand the situation, then they might not be as compatible as she thought. Not giving Jordan time to say anything, she went back to Brady. "Come with me, Brady. Let's get you cleaned up and warm." She coaxed him into standing, and with her arm around his waist, she walked him to the spare bedroom. Doctor or not, he needed emotional support.

Crystal helped him into the bathroom. "Would

you like a shower?" Something normal would help him recover his equilibrium.

"I would, but…" His gaze fell to the floor.

To see this strong man's distress hurt her heart. "Brady, I want to help." She blew out a breath. This wasn't going to be good.

He nodded and released his blanket.

"Those bastards." There were bruises and marks all over his arms. His clothing was torn. It was obvious he'd been fighting for his life. Anger welled up in her. Anger at Brady's family, anger at her own, anger that the world couldn't accept people who were different.

"I fought back, but they ganged up on me."

His words sent an arrow straight into her gut. "I'm sure you did." She put her arm around his shoulders. "Brady, I know this is hard, but will you allow me to take some pictures? This needs to be documented."

"No police." His voice ratcheted up a notch.

His fear permeated her skin. Poor guy was scared to death. "Brady, they committed a crime."

"I know they did." His voice was growing stronger. "But this is exactly what they want me to do. I refuse to give into their demands."

Crystal blew out a breath. She'd look up what she could on her phone while Brady was in the shower. They might not have a choice about calling the police. She took out her cell from her pocket. "I'll take them. It's strictly to have them if you change your mind once this is done."

Brady nodded.

Crystal adjusted her camera settings to show time and date. She quickly took pictures of his injuries and his clothing. "Go ahead and shower. I'll find you something clean to wear."

He nodded. Crystal stepped out of the bathroom to allow him some privacy.

Once alone, she quickly brought up state laws about mandatory reporting. She blew out a breath. It was up to Brady if he wanted to report it or not. She walked back into the living room where Sage and Jordan stood toe to toe.

"Don't you get it, Jordan? They did this to him."

"I do get it, but I'm not sure how this is going to impact our case, and we need to report it."

"I don't give a flying fuck about our case. This is Brady. My Brady."

"Excuse me," Crystal kept her voice even. They looked at her. "Sage, do you have something Brady can wear? He's taking a shower."

"Crystal, this isn't wise. We have to get Brady out of here. Or at least call the police."

"No, we don't." Crystal stared at Jordan with her arms crossed over her chest. "Brady has the right not to involve the police. Right now, he needs help. He feels safe here, and his needs come before anything else."

Sage gave Crystal a little smile. Crystal took it as one of gratitude.

"My bedroom is the door on the right. There's some of Brady's things in the dresser, second and third drawers," Sage said.

"Thank you." Crystal turned.

"Crystal," Jordan said. "This won't look good."

"I don't care. Brady and Sage need our help as friends, not as her lawyer and her lawyer's paralegal. Damn it, Jordan. They're your friends too."

"Yes, they are." He drew his hand through his hair. "I'm not trying to be an ass. I have to consider the legal ramifications."

Her spine stiffened. "Deal with it," she said and left. There was no way Crystal wasn't going to help Brady. Not when she knew what he was going through. She found his clothing and went back into the guest bedroom.

"Brady, I have some clean clothes for you," she called out.

"Thank you." His voice was firm.

"Shall I leave them on the bed for you?" The bathroom door opened. Crystal breathed a sigh of relief to see Brady had a towel around his waist. She glanced at his back as he walked, no broken skin, but there would be bruising.

Brady dropped the towel, and Crystal turned her back to him. "How much trouble is Sage going to be in?" he asked. "I don't want her to get into trouble. She's mine to protect."

Crystal was startled by his words. He was a sub, yet, he was acting a bit like a Dom. Interesting. "Depends if anyone else finds out." She wasn't going to lie to him. There could be some issues if Brady's family pursued the fact Brady was here. They could even claim Sage did this to Brady. She wasn't going to borrow trouble. Brady and Sage were the victims here.

"Jordan is upset with me."

The rustling of fabric reached her ears. "He'll get over it." He was probably angry with her for defying him, but she couldn't walk away, not from this. "Jordan and Sage are friends, but he is also her lawyer. Men think differently."

"Yeah we do. Maybe I shouldn't have come here. I don't want to get Sage into trouble." Brady's voice was filled with concern.

"Why did you come here?" She was pretty sure she knew the answer but wanted to hear it from him.

"Because I'm safe here." Brady paused. "Sage and I take care of each other. I'm my own man; I have a career and everything. Sage understands that, but she also understands I get tired of making all the decisions all the time. I need someone to take over and let me be me. No concerns or worries."

Safety, love, and acceptance. It was all there in his voice. "It's okay, Brady. We'll figure this out." Somehow they would. She wasn't going to let Brady's family near him, even if it meant defying Jordan and the courts. This was abuse at its core and from his family not Sage.

"I'm dressed now."

Crystal turned around. The t-shirt and shorts hung on his frame. "You've lost weight."

Brady looked down at himself. "Yeah."

Raised voices from the living room made Brady wince. "Give me the towel and I'll put it in the bathroom. Why don't you lie down and rest?" His face was lined with fatigue.

"I should go out there."

"You need to rest. Your body has had a trauma, and rest is the best thing for you. As a doctor, you are aware of what a body needs. Don't worry about Jordan and Sage." Crystal took the towel from his outstretched hand and carried it into the bathroom.

Brady's ripped up clothing lay on the floor. Crystal left the items there. They could be collected later. Right now Brady was her biggest concern. She walked back into the bedroom to find him under the covers. Good, a doctor who could take advice.

Crystal grabbed the chair from the corner and brought it over next to the bed. "I'm here for you." She placed her hand palm up on the bed. Brandy slipped his hand out and placed it in hers. "Rest. No one will hurt you here."

"I like you," Brady said and then began talking. Crystal let him talk, because it would help him.

An hour later, she crept out of the bedroom. Brady had fallen asleep. Her mind was still reeling from his story. When she entered the living room, Jordan was pacing, and Sage glared at him. Jordan stopped pacing when he saw her.

"We have to go," he said. "We can't be caught here. We're aiding and abetting."

"No," she replied quietly.

"No?" His voice was low and hard.

"I'm staying." Crystal glanced at Sage. "Brady is resting. How are you holding up, Sage?"

"Barely. And he doesn't understand." Sage jerked her chin in Jordan's direction.

"I do understand. I'm just not letting emotion get in the way," Jordan declared.

"This is all about emotion," Crystal said. "Come sit down, both of you." She'd listened to Brady and realized how much his life mirrored hers at times. Brady was stronger than any of them thought. He'd explained more about the dynamic between him and Sage. An education for Crystal.

"Crystal," Jordan started.

"Look, emotions are involved. Jordan, you can leave if you want, but I'm staying. Sage needs support and so does Brady." Crystal glared at Jordan. He was going to stay or leave; either way, this was going to happen.

"It's not ethical for us to be here and not report this. The law is being violated."

Her temper flared. "Oh, for fuck's sake!" Crystal waved her hands in a dismissive manner. "Mandatory reporting of abuse is only in the case of children or vulnerable adult. This is about Brady and what his family has done to him. If you sit your ass down, I'll explain what I think we need to do first thing tomorrow morning."

Jordan's mouth dropped open.

"You go, girl," Sage said before taking a seat on the sofa.

Crystal stared at Jordan. If he walked out, then it was over. But his eyes twinkled even as he tried to frown at her. "I'm listening." He marched over and sat down on the sofa.

"Park the attitude, please." She sat down on the chair across from them. "I looked up the law on abuse, and it mainly covers children and vulnerable adults. Brady is neither. He can make his own decisions. So if he says no police, it doesn't mean at a later date he won't want to file assault charges, but he's not required to at this point."

Crystal took a breath. Jordan nodded. "Brady and Sage are engaged in a consensual relationship. Yes, there are archaic laws on the books the family might try to use against them, but when was the last time you saw anyone prosecuted or sued under those laws?"

Jordan ran his hand over his face. "Never."

"Brady's family is using him against Sage. I don't know why they don't like Sage, but they don't. They hurt him, beat him, all because he wants to live his life his way."

"I've never had any contact with his family," Sage said.

"No, but you're involved with their son. There's something there, but I don't know what."

"It's his word against theirs," Jordan commented.

"Stop being an ass," Sage said.

"He's right, Sage." Crystal hated to admit it, but it was true. "To a point," she clarified. "Brady is an adult in the eyes of the law. But I think we can use it. Brady is a submissive, has admitted he submits to Sage, but his family is trying to use his submissive nature against him."

Jordan sat forward. "How?"

"Brady told me he went to his family this morning to try one last time to get them to drop this civil suit. They refused, and when Brady went to leave, his brothers attacked him, and his parents stood by and did nothing."

"He's not going back to them," Sage declared.

"No, but he'll need to go someplace safe." Crystal was running the possibilities through her head. "Once they realize Brady's not at his apartment, I don't trust his family not to stake out your place, Sage."

"Restraining order?" Sage asked.

Crystal shook her head. "Brady would have to file a police report, and it will take a few days to make its way through the court system."

"Our hearing isn't until Wednesday," Jordan said.

"I know. It gives us a few days to get Brady on board and for us to plan for any issues that could come up," Crystal said.

"I'll do whatever you need me to do," Sage said.

"First, we need a place where Brady can stay where no one will find him," Crystal said.

"It can't be anyone from the club," Sage said.

"You don't want the club or Max brought into this," Jordan said.

"I don't. The club is safe space as far as I'm concerned," Sage commented.

Crystal thought for a moment. Who did she know that could take Brady in for a few days? "Excuse me for a minute." Crystal stood up and went into the kitchen. She pulled out her cell phone and dialed. "Hey, Tessa, I have a big favor to ask of you."

"What is it?"

"Can a client stay with you for a few days? I need a place no one will look for him."

"Sure. My spare bedroom is available, and I know you wouldn't be asking if it wasn't important."

"It is. I don't want to give the details over the phone. I'll call you before Jordan and I bring him over."

"With Jordan, huh? Guess last night was a good one."

Crystal blushed. "Yeah. Thanks, you're the best. Call you later." Crystal hung up the phone and walked into the living room. "My friend Tessa has agreed to let Brady stay with her." Sage's eyes grew wide. "No worries, Sage. She won't take advantage of Brady once I explain everything. Tessa never would. She's not that type of person."

"Thank you," Sage said.

"I'm not sure about this," Jordan said.

"It's perfect. No one will associate Brady with Tessa, and he'll have a place he can lay low for a few days."

"I still feel like we're skirting the law and ethics in all this," Jordan commented.

"It's obvious Brady's family has no ethics. I'm not going to let Brady go back to his apartment where they could be waiting. Besides we're not *Brady's* lawyers, and *Brady* didn't file the suit, so we're not violating anything. We're getting Brady out as fast as we can."

"It's a good plan, Jordan," Sage said.

"It is," he admitted. "I may not like this, but it is a solid plan. At least this way, he won't be with Sage or with either of us. Okay, let's get him moved." He lasered Crystal with his gaze. "And then you and I are going to talk."

Crystal quivered at his tone. Well, it didn't matter because Brady was the important one here. She could handle Jordan.

* * * *

"I should paddle your ass for the stunt you pulled," Jordan said when they arrived at his house.

The car ride had been filled with tension. Crystal nodded, but he had to understand this was the best way. She couldn't let Brady go home, not knowing what had happened and her own history with her family. A tremor shook her.

"I know you don't fully agree with me, but I do know where Brady is coming from." She wasn't going to back down on this. It was the right thing to do.

"Really?" Jordan pulled a bottle of beer out of the fridge and waved it at her.

Crystal shook her head. "Alcohol is not the answer." She kept her gaze on him.

The refrigerator door slammed shut, and Jordan glared at her. "You're right; it's not." He held two bottles of water in his hand.

"Let's go sit down." Crystal waved her hand toward the living room.

"I still want to paddle your ass."

"Maybe later." She was handling his anger with a determination she didn't know she had. Seconds later, it hit her. She trusted Jordan. He wouldn't hurt her like her family had. He was a good man, and once he stopped thinking like a lawyer, he'd get it.

His brown eyes flashed with desire. Crystal sat down on the sofa, curling one leg beneath her, and she turned so she could face Jordan. He faced her when he sat down.

Crystal took a deep breath. "I've told you a bit about my family." Jordan nodded. "I understand what Brady is going through because I've been through it myself." Well, at least she got the words out. Her stomach was churning, but it had to be said. She wanted Jordan to understand why she'd done what she did.

"What do you mean?" He frowned.

"I mean, when I was younger, my father beat the crap out of us kids for not doing what they wanted us to." She hadn't mentioned the beatings to him before. Now was the time to come clean and put her fears to rest.

"They fucking abused you." Jordan's voice grew hard; his body tensed.

"Yes." She wasn't going to sugar coat it anymore. Seeing Brady and what happened to him today had opened the floodgates. "It's one of the reasons I left at eighteen."

"What about your brothers and sisters?" Jordan shifted toward her.

"They seemed not to care." She shook her head. "Maybe they did. I don't know. I learned to hide who I was and how I felt." A quake shook her body.

"Baby." Jordan took her hand. "Why didn't you tell me before?"

"I wasn't ready, but seeing Brady and his determination, I knew I wouldn't hide it from you anymore." She paused for a breath. "I was taught to submit to their ideals. To adhere to a strict belief system I never could understand. But because of it, I've been afraid of my sexuality since I was a teenager. If they thought I was having impure thoughts, they'd throw me in the sin closet. I was taught sex was dirty and no *good girl* would want to have sex." Everything from her past had come to the forefront. Time to exorcise some personal demons.

"Pure rubbish."

She gave him a small smile. "But I didn't learn that for a long time. In fact, it still affects me."

"And the boyfriends you had?"

"I froze up on them. The old tapes played through my head." She pulled her hand from his and stood up. She couldn't sit still and tell this.

"But you didn't freeze up with me."

"No." She tilted her head as she looked at him. "You got under my skin from the first time we met."

"I could say the same about you."

"Anyway, today when I saw Brady, I also saw me." She took a deep breath. "I was fifteen, and a boy at school kissed me on the cheek. It was so sweet, so pure."

"What happened?"

She closed her eyes and wrapped her arms around her waist. "One of my brothers saw and told our father. That night, my father and brothers came into my bedroom, my brothers held me down while my father beat me."

"Where the hell was your mother?"

"Right there with my sisters, telling them I had sinned, and this is what happened to sinners." Crystal shook her head, trying to dispel her mother's voice.

"Honey," Jordan stood up, but Crystal held her palm out.

She needed to get this out. "My father was careful not to break the skin, but my entire back was one big bruise for weeks. I could barely walk without being in pain."

"People had to notice."

"They did. My parents said I fell out of a tree."

"Wasn't there anyone you could go to?"

"I wish." Tears gathered behind her eyes. She'd been so afraid no one would believe her. "I wasn't close to anyone. I didn't dare tell a teacher or a neighbor. They were all friends with my parents."

"Couldn't you have gone to the police?"

She shook her head. "I was too scared of the consequences if I did. I was under eighteen; they would have gone to my parents first." Her mind replayed conversation after conversation she overheard at her parents' house. Everything was always the kids' fault, and how they never acted like they should.

"So you endured." Jordan's soft voice brought her back to the present, his features no longer filled with anger, but with concern.

"I did, but the second I turned eighteen, I was out the door. One thing my parents did believe in was a good work ethic, so I babysat all through high school. Every job I could get. Even with kids no one else would babysit. I hid part of the money so my parents wouldn't take it from me." She took a deep breath. "The day of my eighteenth birthday, I snuck out of the house before dawn. I had a backpack filled with a few clothes, my journal, and money. I bought a bus ticket."

"You were gone before anyone knew it."

"Yes. Because they would have stopped me. They would have come after me; I was sure of that. I waited over a year to contact them and tell them I was okay, but I never told them where I lived. Not even the one time I went back to visit." Crystal opened her eyes and stared at Jordan. "This is what is happening to Brady. His own natural tendencies are being used against him, and I won't let it happen."

"Of course not." Jordan crossed the room and pulled her into his arms. "You are not that type of person. I'm sorry if it seemed like I wasn't listening."

"You were listening, just not hearing. All you could think about were the legal ramifications, and I understand."

He held her close. "You saw the emotional side of what was going on."

"I did. And once we get Brady on board, it's the emotional side we can defeat his family with."

"I hope you're right." He stared down at her. "Come on. Let's go to bed and get some sleep. I think we can both use it."

"I should go home."

"No. Tonight you need someone to hold you, and that's going to be me."

He was right. When the nightmares came, Jordan's warmth and comfort kept her from being afraid. She had someone who believed in her. Who loved her for who she was.

Chapter Eight

Monday and Tuesday were busy days. Crystal and Jordan spent their time going over legal briefs and arguments for court. When the day ended, she would go over to Tessa's and talk to Brady. Maybe it was a tad bit unethical…all right, a lot unethical. She wasn't his lawyer, but she needed to advise Brady of their plan. As always, she would make sure Tessa was present in case someone wanted to say she or Jordan coaxed Brady.

"I'm totally on board," Brady declared, his voice strong. He glanced at Tessa, then back to Crystal. "I'm sorry you had to see me the way I was the other day."

"Hey, it's okay." She patted his shoulder. "I'm glad you had someone you could go to."

"I'm a thirty-year-old man. I shouldn't have fallen apart."

"Bull." Crystal wasn't going to let him think that. "Brady, what your family did is reprehensible. You were in shock, something I understand well."

"How?"

Crystal glanced at Tessa. "Tessa, I'm swearing you to secrecy until I'm ready to tell Sierra."

"What?" Tessa looked shocked.

"Please." Crystal knew she was asking a lot, but for right now, she needed to do this.

"I'll keep it to myself," Tessa said as she reached over and took Crystal's hand.

"My family is a lot like yours; they don't understand our life choices. I'm glad you had Sage to go to. When my father beat me, I had no one." Tessa's hand tightened around hers, and Crystal squeezed back.

"Your father raised a hand to you?" Brady's features tightened, his eyes darkening.

"He did." She swallowed. "The point I'm making is that I understand about family. I know you don't want to press charges, and I get it."

"Thank you. Do you still see your family?"

"No. There's an advantage. They live in Kansas, so we're not even in the same state."

"But mine are." Brady looked out the window of Tessa's apartment. "I get what you're saying. They're not going to leave me alone even if we do win the case?"

"Maybe, and maybe not. I want you to prepare yourself. Seeing them in court tomorrow isn't going to be fun, and it will be difficult to stare your family down."

"I can do it. For me and for Sage."

Twenty minutes later, Tessa gave Crystal a big hug, and then Crystal left the apartment. Crystal drove to Jordan's home feeling better than she had in days. She'd faced her ghosts.

* * * *

"How's Brady? Is he ready?" Jordan asked over dinner.

"He is." Crystal pushed her food around on her plate.

"What is it, baby?"

"I'm not hungry."

Jordan frowned, but he didn't press; instead, he wrapped up her food and put it in the fridge. He pulled her from the chair and led her into the bedroom.

175

"Shower," he said, pushing her into the bathroom.

When she emerged, Jordan had turned down the sheets, and a bottle of oil sat on the nightstand.

"Come lay down on your stomach, baby." He patted the mattress.

Crystal did as he bid. The scent of roses filled the air right before Jordan's oil-slicked hands touched her back.

"So tense," he murmured as he kneaded her shoulders.

"It's been a long couple of days, and tomorrow is going to be no different." Her eyes drifted shut as Jordan continued to massage her back. His soft voice and his touch were the last things she remembered as she drifted off to sleep.

* * * *

A small smile curved Crystal's lips as she dressed Wednesday morning. Jordan had woken her early with gentle kisses and worked his way into making love. Her skin still tingled from his touch. She hated to leave his bed, but she needed to get home and change.

She slipped on a conservative outfit and put her hair up. After she met Jordan at the office, they went to the courthouse together. Jordan went into the courtroom with Sage. Crystal talked with the bailiff at the door before she went to check on Brady, who waited with Tessa in a nearby room.

She knocked on the door, and Tessa opened it. "Hi." Tessa gave her a hug after letting her in the room.

"Hi." Crystal looked across the room to where Brady paced. "Brady, you ready?"

"Yes." He wore a pair of khaki pants and a white t-shirt. His blond hair was mussed, as if he'd just climbed out of bed. His hands shook.

"It will be all right." She hoped her words helped calm him. "When they're ready for Brady, I'll have a bailiff come get you both."

"Okay." Tessa gave her a smile.

Crystal walked over to Brady. "May I hug you?" Brady nodded, and Crystal enveloped him in her arms. "I'm here for you."

"Thank you," he whispered.

She released him with a smile and walked back to the courtroom. When she stepped inside, she saw Brady's family huddling with their lawyer. She moved to the front row and leaned down between Sage and Jordan. "Everything is ready."

Jordan nodded, and Sage gave a tight smile. Crystal straightened, and everyone stood as the judge came in, then sat. Immediately, the other lawyer stood up. "Your Honor, we have an issue."

"What would that be, Mr. Winters?"

"Mr. Jacobs is missing," the lawyer said.

"And that woman has him," Brady's father stood up and pointed at Sage.

"Control your client, counselor," the judge said and turned to Jordan. "Mr. Frost."

"Yes, Your Honor." Jordan stood up.

"Do you know where Brady Jacobs is?"

"Yes, Your Honor, I do."

"See. I told you," Brady's father yelled.

The judge banged the gavel. "This is a warning, Mr. Jacobs. One more outburst and I'll hold you in contempt." The judge turned his gaze back to Jordan. "Explain."

"Your Honor, Mr. Jacobs arrived at my client's

home on Sunday morning, beaten, bruised, and with his clothing torn. My client called me immediately. I went over with my paralegal."

"Did you call Mr. Jacobs' family?"

"No, sir, I didn't. Mr. Jacobs asked that we not notify his family and made it clear to us he was in no condition to deal with them. Mr. Jacobs informed us his family, the very same family who brought the abuse case against my client, are the ones who inflicted his injuries."

Brady's father jumped up, as did his brothers. The judge glared at them, and their lawyer waved them back into their seats.

"You have proof?" the judge asked.

"We have Mr. Jacobs' word, plus we have photographic evidence."

"And where is Mr. Jacobs now?"

"Waiting in one of the conference rooms down the hall. He's willing to testify, Your Honor. He wants to set the record straight, regardless of what his family wants."

Winters jumped to his feet. "I object, Your Honor. This is unethical."

The judge stared at the lawyer. "This case has been unusual from the start." He looked back and forth, from defendant to plaintiff. "I'm going to allow it. Mr. Jacobs has a right to have his views heard. Mr. Frost?"

That was her cue. Crystal turned and nodded to the bailiff at the back of the room. He left and returned a few minutes later with Tessa and Brady. Brady was trembling. Crystal yearned to go to him, but she couldn't. She smiled and nodded her encouragement.

Brady came down the aisle closest to the wall, away from his family. He stopped next to the front row.

He stared at Sage until the judge spoke.

"Mr. Jacobs, I understand you wish to testify?" the judge said.

"Yes, sir." His voice wobbled, but it was strong.

"Very well, please take the stand." The judge gestured to the witness box. Brady looked at Crystal, and she nodded.

Tessa sat down as Brady entered the witness box. His family glared at him, but Brady kept his attention on Jordan and Sage. Once Brady was sworn in, Jordan stood up.

"Mr. Jacobs, please tell the court how you feel about this whole process?"

"Objection. This has no relevance."

The judge sighed.

"Your Honor, I think this has great relevance. It is Mr. Jacobs' life."

"Agreed. Overruled."

"You haven't heard the full objection," Brady's family lawyer complained.

"I have agreed to let Mr. Jacobs testify. Mr. Frost is asking for his opinion."

"But his opinion is biased," the lawyer said.

Crystal barely prevented herself from rolling her eyes.

"Overruled. Go ahead, Mr. Jacobs."

"I don't agree with my family at all. What Sage and I have is consensual."

"Objection. It's obvious he's been brainwashed," the lawyer said a hint of desperation in his voice.

"You have not presented any such evidence. Overruled."

"Mr. Jacobs," Jordan said. "Can you tell us the

events that led you to my client's home on Sunday?"

Brady's hand trembled as he ran it over his face. "I've been trying to get my family to understand about my relationship with Sage. They refuse to listen. Sunday, I told them I'd had enough, I wasn't going to put up with them any longer."

Crystal's heart swelled. It took courage for Brady to renounce his family.

"What happened when you told them?"

"Objection. What relevance does this have to the case?"

"Your Honor," Jordan said. "Mr. Brady's family brought this case in which they made several allegations that Mr. Brady has vehemently denied. Mr. Brady is an adult and has not been found to be incompetent; therefore, we maintain he has a right to have his opinion heard."

"Agreed. Overruled. Continue."

Crystal kept an eye on Brady's family. They were talking among themselves and to the lawyer. She had a bad feeling about this. As Jordan turned back to Brady, one of his brothers stood. She motioned to Jordan.

"Your Honor," Jordan said. "I ask that no one be allowed to leave the courtroom at this time."

Crystal sighed. She was so glad they'd talked about this. She'd had a feeling Brady's family might try something underhanded.

The judge stared at the brothers. "Sit back down. Bailiff, please make sure no one leaves."

"Yes, Your Honor."

Jordan glanced back at Crystal and nodded.

"Mr. Jacobs, please continue," Jordan said.

"Sunday morning, I told my family enough. I was

leaving when my brothers attacked me.”

Brady’s family erupted, and the judge banged his gavel. “This courtroom will have order, or I will hold you all in contempt.”

“Your Honor, surely you can understand why my clients are upset,” Winters said, waving his hand at Brady’s parents and brothers.

“Get them under control, counselor.” The judge turned to Brady. “I’m going to question the witness.”

Brady was clearly nervous but stayed strong, his attention lasered on the judge. Crystal had warned him his family would go nuts, and the judge might ask him questions.

“Tell me about your relationship with the defendant.”

Brady swallowed. “Sage is wonderful to me. We enjoy each other and give the other what they need.” He smiled at Sage. “Our relationship has a sexual component that includes kink.”

“Kink?” the judge said. “You’re in an alternative lifestyle?”

“Yes, sir.”

“You do realize your family has brought a civil lawsuit for abuse?”

“Yes, sir. I don’t agree, and I refuse to play a part in my family’s pettiness. Sage does not abuse me. We have a loving relationship.”

“I see.” The judge looked over at Brady’s family. “Mr. and Mrs. Jacobs, you claim your son has been abused. I remind you that you are still under oath.”

Brady’s father stood up. “He has. That woman has beaten him.”

“She has not,” Brady yelled, then looked at the

judge. "I'm sorry, sir."

The judge nodded. "Brady, how long have you been in this relationship?"

"Two years."

"I see. Have you lived at home all this time?"

"No, sir. I've been living on my own since I was twenty-five."

"Are you employed?"

"Yes, sir. I'm a physician. I'm starting my own clinic."

"Like hell," his father said.

The judge glared at the family before turning back to Brady. "Brady, tell me more about how you ended up on the defendant's doorstep on Sunday."

"As I stated, I was tired of my family not listening to me. I wanted to give them one last chance to drop this case, so I stopped by my childhood home. I stated the facts and then got ready to leave when my brothers grabbed me and began beating on me."

"I have to object," Winters interjected.

The judge waved his hand in the air. "Overruled. Continue please."

Brady swallowed. "When they were finished, it took me a little bit to get my body to work. I had my keys in my pocket, so I made my way to my car and went to Sage."

"Why the defendant's house?"

"Because I knew I would be safe with her."

"I see." The judge turned his gaze to Sage. "Ms. Montgomery."

"Yes, Your Honor," Sage stood up.

"When Brady showed up at your home, what did you do?"

Sage took a deep breath. "I brought him into my home, wrapped him in a blanket, and then called Mr. Frost."

"Mr. Frost, how long was it from the time Ms. Montgomery called you until you arrived at her home?"

"About forty-five minutes, your honor," Jordan answered.

"I see. Was there anyone else with you?"

"I was, Your Honor." Crystal stood up. "Mr. Frost and I arrived together."

"Ms. Hayden, what did you see?"

Crystal's heart pounded. "Brady was huddled on the sofa. Mr. Frost explained right away about the legal ramifications."

"Did that stop you?"

"No. Sorry, Your Honor, but I was worried about Brady."

"Why were you worried about him?"

"I could see the fear in his face."

"See? She beat him, not us. We told you," Brady's father yelled.

"This is your last warning. One more outburst, Mr. Jacobs, and you will be escorted from this courtroom and jailed on a contempt charge. Am I clear?"

Winters answered for him. "Yes, Your Honor." He glared at his clients with the clear message to keep quiet.

"What did you do?"

"I took Brady into the spare bedroom, helped him clean up and talked with him while Jordan and Sage talked."

"What did Mr. Jacobs tell you?"

"He told me about how he didn't want this case

against Sage, that his family was doing it out of spite. They hated his lifestyle. He'd told them Sunday morning he was done trying to get them to understand, then his brothers beat him up. He came where he was safe."

"Your Honor," Winters said. "Ms. Hayden works for the defense. She's naturally going to protect her client."

"I understand that, Mr. Winters. But she's also a witness." The judge turned back to her. "Ms. Hayden, as a paralegal you're aware of the consequences of lying in court.

"Yes, Your Honor. I'm willing to take the oath if need be."

The judge nodded. "Were you aware of the type of relationship your client and Brady had?"

"Yes, Your Honor."

"Did it bother you?"

"Maybe at first." She wasn't going to lie even though Mr. Winters beamed. "I also believed it could be considered abuse. But as I learned more about the lifestyle, I realized I had some misconceptions. It's all about consent between adults."

"Thank you, Ms. Hayden." The judge looked at Brady. "Brady, you may step down and sit wherever you choose."

Brady left the stand and sat down next to Crystal. She squeezed his hand.

"I'm going to take a ten minute recess before I render my decision. Everyone stays in the courtroom." The judge stood and left.

"What does this mean?" Sage asked quietly.

"It looks like he's going to put an end to this one way or the other. I hope he's going to rule in our favor,"

Jordan said.

Brady's family began talking furiously between themselves. Several times they glared at them, but Crystal didn't care. Tessa smiled at Brady and told him he did a good job.

The ten minutes seemed like ten hours. They all stood as the judge came back in. "Please be seated," the judge said. "This has been an unusual case from the beginning." He looked at Brady's family, his expression cold and controlled. "Brady is of legal age. He has the right to live as he chooses."

Brady's hand tightened around Crystal's.

"Per the testimony of both parties, the relationship between Brady Jacobs and Sage Montgomery is consensual, and they are both adults.

"As to this civil matter, it is the finding of this court that there is no case since the plaintiff has not established that any abuse has occurred. Therefore, this case is hereby dismissed."

Brady's family erupted, and Mr. Winters started talking.

The judge banged his gavel several times. "Mr. Winters, get your clients under control."

"We will be appealing, judge," Winters said.

"Feel free, but my ruling stands. Mr. Brady Jacobs is free to be with Ms. Montgomery." The judge addressed Brady's family. "Mr. Jacobs, your son has grounds to pursue charges of assault, which is a very serious felony. I would strongly advise you to consider your options carefully at this point. Your son is an adult and, as I said before, has the right to live his life as he chooses. If you pursue another civil action, Ms. Montgomery could very well countersue for harassment.

Think long and hard about your next move, sir. This court is adjourned."

The judge stood and left the room.

"Did we win?" Brady asked quietly.

"We did." Crystal smiled at Brady.

* * * *

Saturday night, Crystal took a deep breath before going into the club with Jordan. After winning the case, they went out with Sage and Brady to celebrate, then agreed to meet at the club on Saturday night.

Crystal was happy for her new friends but, at the same time, wondered what it meant for her and Jordan. Their working time was almost at an end.

The club was already crowded when they arrived. Jordan pulled her aside. "I know we've been talking about it, but I need to hear your choice. Do you want to play in the club tonight?"

Her skin tingled. They *had* been talking about this until the case took over. Was she ready for this? An anxious quiver ran through her body, but she trusted Jordan more than anyone else. Yes, she was. "I'm ready."

"Are you okay with having your breasts exposed?"

Crystal closed her eyes. She could do this. "Yes, my breasts, not my pussy." He knew she didn't want to be nude.

"Not until you're ready. I can still tease you with your clothes on."

She smiled up at him. "I know you can. But I'm okay with the top."

"I'll let Max know we'll need one of the areas later." He brushed a kiss over her nose. "I see Sierra is with Sage and Brady. Why don't you go say hello."

He turned her, and she saw her friends.

"Okay, don't be long." She gave his hand a squeeze and joined them.

* * * *

Jordan found Max. "Congrats on winning," Max said, shaking his hand.

"Thanks. It was really a non-case, but it's always tricky when kink is involved. Plus, you never know with the judge."

"I can't believe the judge was so open," Max said.

"Yeah, well, I got a call from the judge. He doesn't fully understand kink, but he called a friend who did. It's amazing how small the community is."

"It is."

"I want to reserve one of the scene stations for tonight."

"You and Crystal?"

He nodded. "She's ready. Is the spider web open?"

"Isn't the web a little hard core for a first timer?" Max asked.

"I'm going to tease her. This way, she's standing, and I can keep her attention on me."

"Good idea. I'll put you down at eleven."

"Perfect. It will give us time to mingle and watch a few scenes. And by the way, the gate was open again tonight." They'd had some issues with the gate being open rather than closed. "I thought it was fixed."

"I know. The gate company is coming out again on Monday. I told them if they don't fix it right this time, they're going to put in a brand new one."

Jordan laughed. "I bet that will light a fire under them."

"The owner himself is coming out with the crew to see what the issue is. Ralph is staying on the desk all night to make sure no one wanders in who shouldn't be here."

"Good." Jordan glanced over at the group. "It's good to see Brady and Sage happy."

"I was beginning to worry, but it is." Max sighed as a Dom walked up to them. "Excuse me, Master Max, but there's a situation with one of the stations."

Jordan slapped Max on the shoulder and made his way over to Crystal.

* * * *

Crystal was nervous when Jordan led her up to a big round metal frame with what looked like a spider web in the middle. She'd witnessed a scene here, and she wasn't ready for the web.

"Umm, Sir." She tugged on his hand.

"Yes, sweetheart." Jordan turned to her. In an instant, he had her in his arms. "Baby, what is it?"

"I don't think I'm ready for it, Sir." She gestured toward the equipment.

"You're not." He smiled. "I'm going to tie you to it. Trust me to know what you're ready for or not."

Crystal took a deep breath. Jordan wouldn't do something he was aware she wasn't ready for. "Sorry, Sir. I wasn't thinking."

"You were unsure, and I'd rather you ask than panic." He dropped a kiss on her forehead and led her up the two steps and onto the small stage.

Jordan's bag was waiting for him, and a covered metal table stood near the wheel. "Come here." He pulled her to him. "Safe words?"

"Red to stop, yellow to slow down, Sir."

"If things get too intense, don't hesitate to use them."

She nodded.

"And be as vocal as you want. I want to, need to hear you. Every cry of pleasure makes me happy."

"Yes, Sir." Oh goodness, she was going to do this. Excitement with a tinge of apprehension slid through her veins.

"Now, let's get you out of your top." He began to undo the lace babydoll-type top she'd worn at his request. When he finished, he folded it and placed it next to his bag, pulled out a set of restraints, and led her over to the wheel.

"I'm going to restrain your arms and legs. Your feet will be on the floor."

"Yes, Sir." Crystal tried to settle her nerves. Jordan had restrained her before, mainly at home.

He took her left arm and put it into position.

"Sir?"

"Yes, sweet."

"This is different, Sir." He had her arm out to the side rather than over her head.

"I don't want your arms to go numb. This will help." He fastened one and then the other. "Okay?"

"Green, Sir." They'd talked about this as well. He would check in with her often. She was glad because, sometimes, when his loving overwhelmed her, her mind went blank.

Jordan knelt down and secured her feet, then crossed over to his bag. He dangled a blindfold in front of her. It was a soft limit for her.

"We didn't talk about this, but it will heighten your sensations and help you forget where you are."

She swallowed.

"What is it, my sweet?"

Leave it to him to notice her apprehension. "I'm not sure, Sir."

"Talk to me." He leaned close, and she fought to catch her breath.

"It's just…it was dark when my parents threw me into the sin closet." She hated the tremor in her voice.

His lips tightened. "I see. We don't need it." He started to turn away.

"Sir." There had been brief disappointment in his gaze, then understanding. Crystal lifted her chin. "It's fine, Sir." She took a deep breath.

"No, sweetheart. Not if it's going to remind you of a horrible situation. One that no one should ever have to go through."

"Please, Sir." It was time to stop letting her past control her and her feelings. "I want to try."

Jordan nodded and slipped the blindfold on.

The leather clung to her skin and cut out all light. Jordan ran his fingers over her cheek and down her neck. Crystal shivered.

"Are you okay?"

"Yes, Sir. I'm fine."

"So courageous," he whispered, then his touch was gone.

She took deep breaths to calm her racing heart and to see if she could hear him. Instead, she heard voices. Lots of voices. Oh yeah, they were in the club. She'd almost forgotten.

Oh crap, anyone could see her breasts. She tried to hunch her shoulders but couldn't. She jumped when a hand landed on her shoulder.

"Easy, sweet, it's me." Her tense muscles relaxed with the sound of Jordan's soft voice. "It's just you and me."

He trailed his fingers over her collarbone and between her breasts. Then he made circles around her breasts.

Her nerves quivered with anticipation.

"That's it. Relax and let me arouse you."

She sucked in a breath when he splayed his palm over her belly, the tips of his fingers brushing the pair of shorts she wore.

"Pale skin against mine." He continued to caress her as he talked.

Her breasts grew heavy, and her nipples grew hard. What was he waiting for? Her skin pebbled with goosebumps under his touch. The anticipation was killing her.

Then his touch was gone, and she moaned. Jordan chuckled. Something new glided over her skin. He was twirling it over her neck and then over her nipples.

"What is it, Sir?" she asked.

"Concentrate and tell me." He went from one breast to the other. Her breathing increased with the sensations over her skin. Whatever this was, it was light and tickled.

"Feathers, Sir."

"Yes, it's a feather duster."

He swirled it over her stomach, and then down her legs, before taking it away. He was back within moments. Jordan pinched her nipples, and she couldn't suppress a small scream.

"Easy, sweet." His breath whispered against her skin. "Are you ready for this?"

"What, Sir?"

"Remember what we talked about last night and what I wanted to do to these pretty nipples."

Crystal sucked in a breath. "You mentioned nipple clamps, Sir." Oh God. Part of her wanted to try, another part wanted to yell her safe word.

"I did. Since you can't see, I'll explain the pair I have. Think about a pair of tweezers with rubber on the ends and a round disk you push to make the tweezers close. That's what I'm going to use on you, sweet."

"Yes, Sir." Her pussy tightened.

Jordan plucked her nipple until it was almost painfully hard, then he applied the first clamp. As he tightened it, she thought it wasn't so bad, until it was almost too tight.

"Yellow, Sir."

"Very good." The pressure eased slightly. Then he applied the second one. This time, she didn't have to call out her safe word.

Her nipples were so tight and needy. Her pussy clenched, and she shifted her hips.

"Oh yes, the clamps are making you hot already, aren't they?"

"Yes, Sir."

"What about now?" His tongue flicked one nipple, and she cried out as her hips bucked. He did the same with the other one, and her body shook. "Oh yes, do you want to know what I see, sweet?"

Did she want to know? "Yes, Sir." She wanted to hear from his lips what he was seeing.

"Your skin is flushed a pretty, dark pink. Your nipples are hard little beads. You keep shifting your hips. I bet if I slipped my hand into your shorts I'd find you wet.”

His words increased the heat flowing through her veins. “You would, Sir.”

“Your arousal is music to my soul. Let’s see, what should I use next?”

Next? Wasn’t he done yet? No, he wasn’t. She should know better; the man had teased her before. Maybe not to this extent, but damn, he loved playing with her.

Something soft tickled the top of her foot, then moved up one leg, down the other, and back up. Then he ran it over her arms, letting her feel every inch of it.

Whatever the toy was, it was soft, but there were—tails. She trembled when he ran it over her breasts, teasing her nipples where the clamps still drove her nuts. He reached her hip and gave her a gentle swat.

Her body shook. “Flogger, Sir?” She hadn’t expected the soft caress to her skin.

“A very special flogger.” He flicked it against her other hip. “This is a rabbit fur flogger.”

The strands snapped against her abs, and she sucked in a breath. It didn’t hurt. There was a little sting to it, enough to awaken every nerve ending with each strike. Jordan teased her back and forth, the flogger, then the feather, his touch.

She had no idea how much time had passed. He removed the nipple clamps. Heat and exquisite pain flooded her body. Crystal opened her mouth, breathing heavy.

“Okay, baby?” Jordan asked.

“I need a minute, Sir.” The pain faded leaving behind pure pleasure flowing from her nipples to her pussy. “I’m good now, Sir.”

Jordan teased her nipples with the flogger. Her body was one big nerve. Each touch of his hand or a toy sent lightning to her clit. Her pussy throbbed.

"Please, Sir," she whispered.

"Please what, my sweet?"

She didn't know. Did she want him to stop? Not until he was ready. She moaned as he blew on her nipples. They tightened further. "Oh, Sir." Her toes curled. "I think I'm going to climax."

"You may come all you want, my sweet, though it doesn't mean I'll stop."

Crystal wasn't sure how long she could hold out, but she didn't want to orgasm until he was through with her.

"Let's see if this cools you off."

She squealed as something freezing touched her belly. Crystal jerked in the restraints and shivered. Instead of cooling her off, it pushed her need higher.

"Let it all go, my sweet," he whispered in her ear. "Let your body go. Come for me."

"Sir." Her body trembled.

"I want you to come. I want you to come apart from my touch, my toys." He pinched one nipple and then the other. "Come baby."

Crystal screamed as her climax overwhelmed her. She trembled from head to toe. Her pussy clenched, and her clit pulsed as her orgasm went on and on. She began to float away on a cloud.

* * * *

Jordan smiled as he watched Crystal climax and then as her face went lax. She was likely in subspace. He'd wondered if he could get her there. Jordan stood in front of her and kissed her softly. "So perfect." He bent over and undid her ankle restraints, then, keeping his knee between her legs, he undid her arms. She slumped into his embrace.

"Take her to the aftercare area. I've got this," Max told him.

"Thanks." Jordan lifted Crystal into his arms and carried her off the stage, where Sierra waited with a blanket. He smiled as he took it. Their friends were the best. He sat on one of the aftercare sofas with Crystal in his lap, the blanket wrapped around her.

Jordan slipped the blindfold off and tucked it in his pocket. Crystal's breathing was a little rapid, but her color had returned to normal after being fully flushed while he'd played with her.

God, this woman was one of a kind. She reacted to him like no other he'd ever played with. She was finally releasing her sensuality and letting him see the sexual woman underneath.

He held her close, keeping his gaze on her face. While the case they'd been working on might be over, he wasn't going to let her out of his life.

"I can feel you staring at me." Her words were soft.

"How are you doing?" He ran his fingers over her cheek, and she trembled. "Are you cold?" He glanced around to see if he could get someone's attention to get him another blanket.

"I'm not cold." Her voice was still dreamy. "Your touch made me shake. My nerves are hyper-sensitive right now."

He grinned. "How did you like your first public scene?"

"I liked it." Her green eyes flashed like gems.

"The blindfold helped me relax. I forgot all about our audience."

"Good. You went into subspace. How did that feel for you?" He shifted her on his lap.

"I was drifting on a cloud, if that's what you're asking." She shifted, and his cock twitched. "Do you need some attention?"

"No." He lowered his forehead to rest against hers. "This is all about you."

"When we get home?"

Home? It was the first time she called his place home. "If you're feeling up to it."

"Oh, I will be." Her eyes twinkled.

"Witch." He took her lips with his, and when they finally parted, they were both breathing heavily. "Rest a bit. And then we'll mingle a little before we go."

"Yes, Sir." She laid her head on his shoulder and closed her eyes.

Jordan smiled. This was his woman. He was falling for her. His heart pounded. When had he started falling for her? Probably the night they all went to coffee, when she wanted to protect the little boy. The more time they spent together, the more she crept into his heart and his life.

He didn't mind it all. Crystal fit in his work and his life. She might think everything was over when the job was, but he wasn't about to let her get away. He wasn't falling for her. It was much, much more than that. He loved her.

* * * *

"How did you like being blindfolded?" Jordan asked as he dried Crystal off after their shower. Her skin seemed to still be glowing in the aftermath of their play.

"Once I got out of my head, it was enjoyable."

He grinned. "That's the point. Get you out of your normal thought patterns and rely on touch, sound, and emotion."

"Were you testing me with the nipple clamps to see if I'd safeword out?"

"Yes and no." He nudged her out of the bathroom. "I wanted to test your pain tolerance but also wanted to see how far I could go."

"And my calling out yellow?"

"Was exactly what I wanted. You told me to slow down, and I did. Remember, communication is important." He would continue to reinforce communication as their relationship went on.

"Yeah." She climbed onto the mattress, and when Jordan laid down, she snuggled into his embrace.

"Did you enjoy the rabbit flogger?" He'd selected it very carefully. Light enough not to mark her skin but enough to cause a slight sting.

"I did. It caused my body to heat, and it didn't hurt." She tilted her head up. "But was using the ice cube, necessary?"

He laughed. "A way to get you to lose the control you were holding onto." Jordan kissed her forehead. The blushing of her skin, the sheen of sweat, her choppy breathing, the way her toes curled, and the breathless moan of pleasure when she climaxed. He wanted to make her do it again and again. "Since you went into subspace, I want you to be prepared for the aftermath."

"Oh?" Her lips touched his jaw.

"Yes. Everyone reacts differently to subspace, but I want to make sure you understand that, if you're feeling down or start crying without reason, it's okay. I'm here to take care of you."

She smiled against his skin. "I'm here to take care of you too." Her words were soft, and then next thing he knew, she was asleep.

Jordan tightened his arms around her. Life would never be boring with Crystal around. And he planned on keeping her.

* * * *

Crystal walked into the office Monday at ten. She and Jordan had overslept, and she needed to go home for clean clothes. She placed the coffee tray on Valerie's desk along with a couple of bags.

"Coffee, breakfast, and something for later," she said to Valerie as she handed her a coffee and set a bag on the desk.

"You've never been late before," Valerie said taking a sip of coffee.

"I overslept." She picked up a coffee tray and bags. Crystal carried everything into her office, before grabbing Jordan's coffee out of the tray. She knocked on Jordan's door and stuck her head inside.

"I hope you brought provisions."

"As if I wouldn't." She walked in with his coffee and breakfast.

"Where is yours?"

"On my desk."

"Bring it in. There's something we need to discuss."

"Sounds serious." She frowned. He'd been in good spirits when he dropped her off at her apartment earlier.

"It is."

Crystal bit her lip, went back to her office, and

picked up her coffee, food, and bag before going back into Jordan's office. Her mind spun over what could make Jordan so serious. She closed his office door before taking a seat.

Her stomach turned over at the grave look on Jordan's face. "What is it?" Thank goodness she hadn't eaten yet.

"Someone followed us on Saturday."

She set her coffee cup on his desk with a trembling hand. "What does that mean?"

"It means they saw us go into the club."

Crystal closed her eyes. Someone saw them. Did they know they went into a BDSM club? *Slut. Whore. Bitch.* Her parents' words slammed around inside her head. Damn it. Those darn tapes had been silent for a while and were now back with a vengeance.

"They don't know what goes on in the club, but they saw Brady and Sage walk in as well," Jordan said.

"His family?" Who else could it be? Why was Brady's family so insistent on making trouble?

"I'm guessing our tail was a PI his family hired to follow us and because of the court case. They're putting two and two together."

"Or that blasted reporter. Damn." Her mind ran through the faces she'd seen on Saturday night. This could be bad, very bad.

"It was Brady's family," Jordan said with certainty.

"Have you told Max yet? Did anyone get inside?" She remembered his comment about how the gate shouldn't have been open.

"I haven't talked to Max yet. He's next on the list. And no, he didn't get inside. As far as I know, he didn't even try. Ralph didn't report anything. I wanted to tell you first because you're named in the letter."

"Letter?" Jordan was notified in writing? Her stomach turned over.

Jordan slid a piece of paper across the desk. Crystal picked it up, and her anger grew as she read it. "Oh fuck no," she said. This was out of bounds and criminal.

The letter from Mr. Winters, the Jacobs' family lawyer, threatened to expose Jordan, her, Sage, and Brady along with the location of the club unless they convinced Brady to return to the family fold. "Don't they understand this is all consensual?"

"Apparently not." He leaned forward. "I'm not concerned for myself; I couldn't care less if someone outs me. It's you and the others I worry about."

"I agree." This could impact everyone associated with the club.

Jordan's cell rang. He looked at the screen and frowned. "Excuse me, I have to get this."

Crystal nodded. She read the letter over again, her mind working out what they could do. Her main fear was somehow word would get back to her family, and they'd find her. She'd had minimal contact with them over the years, but still, if they came here, there could be trouble. For her, for Jordan, for everyone. Crystal shook her head. Silly, she was a grown woman, but her family could act like a cult at times.

"Yes, I see. Thank you."

The defeated tone in Jordan's voice pulled Crystal from her thoughts. She gasped at the devastation on his face. "Jordan, what is it?"

"The parole board voted to release my father from

jail."

Crystal was on her feet to his side. "I'm so sorry." He'd shared with her late one night that his father's parole hearing was coming up. He refused to be in the same room as the man who killed his mother, but this year, as he'd done every year, he made sure the board had his written victim impact statement. The man deserved a lifetime in jail for killing Jordan's mother.

"I am too." He shook his head. "I'll deal with that later. We have to deal with this matter first."

She wanted to tell him everything could wait so they could talk about his father, but she backed off at his closed-down features. Jordan hated talking about his dad, and while she didn't blame him, the club issue seemed to be bothering him more at the moment.

"Why don't you call Max and Damon, and I'll go call Sierra. Have them come here and let's see if we can get a game plan together on how to deal with this letter."

"Good idea." He smiled and some of the tension left his face.

"We probably need to get Brady and Sage in on this as well." Crystal pulled her cell out of her bag as he picked up his. "Hey, Sierra, Crystal. Can you get to Jordan's office right now?"

"What's going on?" Sierra asked.

"I don't want to discuss anything on the phone. Jordan is talking with Max and Damon to have them come in as well."

"This is serious."

"Unfortunately, yes."

"Okay, I should be there in ten minutes. It will take Max a little longer. I think Damon is close, though."

"Thanks. See you soon." She ended the call and

looked at Jordan.

"Max is in town, so he's going to go pick up Damon, and they'll be here shortly." He dialed another number. "Hey, Sage. Can you and Brady come by my office right now? There is something we need to discuss. Thanks." He glanced at Crystal. "They'll be here in fifteen minutes."

"Okay. Why don't we use the conference room?"

"Good idea." He stood up when she did. "I'm sorry I dragged you into this."

"You didn't drag me into anything I didn't want." She traced the lines on his forehead. "As a group, we'll figure this out."

Jordan took her hand in his and kissed her fingers. "We will. Are you okay?"

"I'm fine." But was she? She wasn't sure right now. After they met with everyone, then she'd analyze her feelings. Later she might be able to express her concerns for their relationship. "Let's get some coffee going for everyone."

"You didn't drink yours." He picked up her now cold coffee.

"No." How much should she tell him? Be honest. "My stomach is a little upset with the news." There was more, but until she had time to go through everything, she couldn't explain it to him.

"Crystal." Jordan kept a hold of her hand. "I hate how this has upset you, and this is probably the worst time for this, but I need to say it. I care about you, and I don't want to lose you."

Her heart clenched. "I care about you too." It was true. She did. It was interesting that they both avoided the L word. "Let's get ready for this meeting." She didn't want to get into her feelings right now. Not in the office. Not with all this looming over them.

Thirty minutes later, they were all assembled in the conference room, and Jordan showed the letter to everyone.

"This could cost you business," Max said to Jordan.

"It could, but I doubt it. I'm not worried. My business will survive."

"Damon?" Max asked.

"I'm fine with whatever you want. If you want my honest opinion, I say fuck them and to hell with them"

Sierra burst out laughing, and the men smiled. "That's Damon," Jordan said.

"Honey?" Max looked at Sierra.

"It's dangerous to agree with Damon, but I'm fine if we tell them to go to hell."

"Won't it hurt your job?" Crystal asked.

Sierra shrugged. "I work for a non-profit. I can warn my boss, and if there's a big deal about it, I can quit."

"But you love your job," Crystal said, staring at her friend.

"It's a job. This is about family."

Crystal's heart stuttered. Family. She hadn't been a part of a family who cared about each other in a long time, if ever. Sierra's words filled her heart with joy.

"I'm fine with telling Brady's family they can go fuck off," Max said.

Jordan looked at Sage and Brady; both had been very quiet. "Sage? Brady?"

Brady lifted his chin. "I'm fucking done." His words were quiet.

"Honey." Sage covered Brady's hand, where it sat on the table with hers.

"I've been quiet long enough. My parents and brothers are dead to me. They've been trying to cause trouble at the clinic as well."

"What do you mean?" Jordan asked.

"They're trying to do a hostile takeover of my clinic."

Crystal's eyes widened, and she began making notes. This was not good at all.

"Are they succeeding?" Max asked.

"Not yet. I've been countering everything I can, but they have resources I don't."

"Bull." Damon slapped his hand on the table. "I refuse to give in to their blackmail."

"Why don't we call the police?" Sierra asked.

"No." Brady's voice was firm. "That is exactly what my father wants. Another court case where he can say, 'woe is me'. I'm not giving in to him, not one inch."

Crystal tapped her pen against her mouth. Her stomach was in knots. "What if we have a lawyer draw up a letter," she started, and all eyes turned to her. "A letter states we are well aware of what they're trying to do. Extortion is a felony in the state, and if he continues to go after Brady's clinic and/or reveal this information on us and the club, all of them will be facing multiple counts and never see the light of day after they are prosecuted."

"Will that work?" Max asked.

"It might." Jordan jotted down some notes. "I mean, right now there are seven of us in the room. Not only is it a lot of court cases, but also if the maximum penalty is applied, it's ten years for each count."

"Not to mention damages, if we take the cases to civil court after the criminal trials are finished." Crystal tapped her pen on the tabletop.

Damon whistled. "They could stand to lose big time."

"I like that idea," Sierra said.

"Let's do it," Brady said, and Sage agreed.

"All right. I'll get on it," Jordan said.

"Jordan, I think it would be better coming from another lawyer," Crystal said.

"I agree," Max said. "You're involved. Is there someone you trust who could send this off?"

"You're right. Yes, I know another lawyer I can trust."

"Then do it, and we'll go from there," Max said, pushing back his chair.

They all said their good-byes, and Jordan ushered Crystal back to his office.

"I'm going to get the ball rolling on this. Are you okay?" Jordan asked her.

She nodded out of habit. She was anything but okay at the moment.

Chapter Nine

Crystal finished typing up the last of her notes on Sage's case and sent them to Jordan. She was being a coward by not printing them and walking them to his office.

She grimaced. In the three days since the letter had been sent off to Brady's family, her emotions were in turmoil. Fear, anxiety, and confusion were all jumbled up into a big ball in the pit of her stomach.

Fear her family would find out where she was. Anxiety about the letter they'd sent to Brady's family and if they'd have to fight. Confusion because she was in love with Jordan and she didn't know if he loved her.

A bitter laugh left her lips. Love. Who knew it could happen so fast, especially to her? She never expected to find a man like Jordan.

He remained the bright spot in her days. And nights. She smiled. Last night, as they made love, he'd been so gentle and tender, trying to pull her out of her own head. He knew something was wrong but, thankfully, didn't press her. Sadness filled her. Until she got her head on straight, it wasn't fair to stay with him.

Besides, the job he'd hired her for was done. They hadn't talked about that either. Instead, he'd kiss her or distract her when she tried to speak about it. Not that she blamed him. She didn't want to leave, but it was time.

She needed time to think. Time to figure out her life and how she was going to deal with the old tapes playing in her head. Crystal picked up the letter she'd written earlier today, slipped it into an envelope, and wrote Jordan's name on it. She stood, grabbed her bag, and walked out of her office.

It was lunchtime, and Valerie was out. Crystal shook her head. She was being a big coward by not saying goodbye to Valerie. But if she couldn't talk to Jordan about this, how could she talk to Valerie? Hell, she hadn't even told Sierra or Tessa about her fears or about leaving her job. Crystal stopped at Kendra's office first, knowing she could come back from lunch at any second, put a letter on her desk, then slipped into Jordan's office and placed the letter on his desk. He'd see it when he got back from court later.

Her heart clenched, and she reminded herself she was doing the right thing. She'd fallen hard for Jordan, but until she had her own life cleaned up, she had no right to bring trouble to his doorstep.

With heavy steps, Crystal made her way to the elevator. She was leaving a man she trusted, a man who had shown her sex wasn't a sin, a man she loved with all her heart.

A tear slipped down her cheek, and she brushed it away and stiffened her spine. Once she got her head on straight, she could tell Jordan her feelings but not until then. Otherwise, she'd never know if she'd made the right choice or not.

* * * *

Jordan read the letter once again.

> *Jordan, I'm sorry*
> *I'm not doing this in*
> *person. I can't. I'm asking*

> *you to give me some time to*
> *sort through all my feelings*
> *and emotions around what*
> *has happened. It's not just*
> *Brady's family's threat to*
> *out all of us but other*
> *things. It's honestly about*
> *me. I have issues I need to*
> *work through. I promise,*
> *once I'm done, we'll talk. I*
> *do want you to know you*
> *opened up something in me*
> *I didn't know was there. I*
> *will be in contact. Love,*
> *Crystal.*

He blew out a breath. He'd found the letter a week ago. Jordan picked up his phone, then put it back down.

Crystal asked for time. He tried to give it to her, but he'd already left a dozen messages, letting her know he was here for her. No response. He'd even questioned Sierra, who told him Crystal was dealing with some heavy shit and to give her time.

Jordan rubbed the back of his neck. What was Crystal dealing with? He wanted to help her so much, but it had to be her decision. He wasn't going to force her; that wasn't his way. But damn, this was hard.

He'd made it clear in his messages if she needed to talk or needed him, to call. Silence. Depression settled over him. He missed her. He wanted her back in his life, his arms, his bed. This was more than kink.

Crystal had helped him see he was nothing like

his father. He never lost his temper. Yes, he got angry, but he'd learned to channel his emotion into other actions. BDSM had helped, taught him control, more than he ever realized until Crystal.

A few more days, he could give her a couple more days. Brady's family had backed down. He'd gotten the news from his lawyer. He'd already called Max, Damon, and Sage, now he wanted to share it with Crystal. Sierra would tell Crystal, but he wanted to do it. He wanted to hold her in his arms as he gave her the news.

A knock sounded on his office door. Jordan looked up, surprised to see it was three in the afternoon. Valerie opened the door and stuck her head in. Thanks to Crystal's friendship, and him firing Johnson, Valerie had blossomed and excelled at her job.

"I have a gentleman who wants to see you. He won't give me his name or why. Do you want to talk with him?"

Jordan frowned. "Very well, send him in." Must be someone who was worried about appearances. Not unusual. Jordan stood.

"Thank you," a male voice said. The door was pushed open, and a gray-haired man walked into his office, his dark brown eyes wary. He was an older man, maybe in his late 50s, early 60s.

"Hello, Jordan."

That voice. Jordan stiffened and stood. The man who'd murdered his mother stood in his office. "What the hell are you doing here?" A swirl of emotions flooded him. Funny, a few months ago, it would have been pure anger, but since Crystal… Jordan closed his eyes and took a deep breath before opening them. He wasn't his father.

"I've come to talk with you." Conrad Frost held up his hand when Jordan opened his mouth. "I'm asking you to listen to me."

Jordan stared at him, emotions churning inside him. "Fine." He gestured to one of the chairs before he took his seat behind his desk. He'd let the man say his piece, but nothing would change. Some might say he was being hard-nosed in this matter, but Jordan couldn't help it. This man had killed his mother and left Jordan with nothing.

"Thank you." His father sat down. "You've done well for yourself, and you look good, son." He sighed, the deep, inward breath of a man with a lot on his conscience.

Jordan waited. He couldn't have spoken if he'd wanted to. Anger and sadness flowed through him.

"Let me start by saying I'm sorry you had to witness what happened to your mother."

Jordan stiffened. This was the last thing he expected. "That doesn't bring her back or change the past. And don't ever call me son."

"Nothing excuses what I did. I had a horrible temper, and that night, it got out of control. I don't blame you for testifying against me or for sending me to jail. I deserved it. I've lived with the guilt all these years. I paid the price for my actions. These past years have helped me heal and shown me a new side of myself."

"Great for you, but it doesn't explain why you're here."

"I came to see you and to let you know if you want a relationship, I'm open to it."

Jordan's gut clenched. His anger morphed into indifference. Yes, this man was his biological father, but his dad had been dead for a long time. "I will never forgive you for what you did." He didn't have it in him. "You took not only my mother from me that night, but your actions also meant I lost my father. Will you please leave?" Ambivalence in his voice. He was done. Jordan stood.

"I understand." His father stood up. "You grew up quite well, and I'm happy you didn't inherit my temper." His father turned and left his office.

Jordan fell back into his chair. His mind was churning. He needed to get out of the office. His father. Crystal. It was all so overwhelming to him, and he was always in control. Jordan laughed, the sound sharp and bitter, even cynical in the silent room. His control was shot.

"Valerie," he called on his way out of his office. "I'm leaving. Go ahead and close down early. I'll see you Monday." Once in his car, he drove toward Wicked Sanctuary. He needed to talk to someone.

* * * *

Crystal opened her apartment door to Sierra. She'd talked to her friends, but she hadn't attended girls' night. "Thanks for coming over." Crystal hugged her friend. The time away from Jordan to think had helped Crystal make some hard decisions. About her family and her life.

"Anytime. I'm so glad you called me. We've all been worried." Sierra stared at her.

"I'm sorry you were worried. I had to think everything through." One of the issues was doing something productive about the old tapes playing in her head. Step one had been admitting she needed help; step two was finding someone to help her.

211

The therapist she'd seen every day for the past nine days, including the weekend, helped her see things more clearly and gave her coping tips on what to do when those tapes started playing. She would keep seeing the therapist for a while, but now, she had her head on straight. It was time for step three. Jordan.

"I understand."

"I need your help." This was another part of her therapy, to ask for help when she needed it instead of bottling everything up.

"You got it. What do you need?"

"I want to make a statement tonight. To Jordan." A shiver of excitement slid over Crystal's skin. She was ready to do this.

"It's about time. He's crazy about you."

"I'm crazy about him." A smile curved her lips.

"What took you so long?"

"I had to straighten out my head around my family and this whole letter thing." She took a deep breath. "I wasn't dealing with my emotions in connection to Jordan very well."

"Have you not listened to your messages?"

Crystal ducked her head. "I did." She'd listened to each and every one of them. He understood she needed time, and what she was trying to do and why. How she didn't need to worry he'd wait for her because that's what someone in love does. Yes, he loved her, and he'd wait, because he wasn't letting her go. She'd cried for hours after hearing him confess his love. The hurt and pain in his voice sliced her heart to ribbons. She would make amends.

"Jordan misses you." Sierra took Crystal by the shoulders. "He received a letter from the lawyer. Brady's family dropped their threat.”

“Oh, that’s wonderful.” Crystal almost laughed. She’d made her decisions based on the letter without even knowing the threat had been resolved. It showed her how much she’d grown all because of Jordan. His touch, his belief in her, but most of all, his love. Yes, she felt his love day in and day out. She wasn’t afraid anymore.

“It is. So now what do you want to do?”

“I want you to help me dress for tonight at the club. I want to surprise Jordan, to show him how I feel about him, but I also want him to know I’m his.”

Sierra’s eyes widened.

“I know. I kind of want a grand gesture. I messed up, and I want him to know I trust him.” And more. While she’d told him she wanted to be his sub, she’d come to realize she needed Jordan like she needed air. She wasn’t afraid anymore.

“Do you have some clothing in mind?”

“I bought some new stuff. It’s on my bed.” Crystal wiped her hands on her jeans. “I’m nervous. What if Jordan doesn’t want me anymore?”

“You have to be kidding.” Sierra hugged Crystal. “If he doesn’t, I’ll kick him in the balls.”

Crystal burst out laughing.

“I mean it,” Sierra said. “He’s lucky to have you. Now, show me your outfit.”

Crystal took Sierra into her bedroom where the outfit she’d bought was laid out.

“Oh wow.” Sierra picked up the sheer skirt and top.

“I wanted to make a statement.”

“Honey, you will.” Sierra smiled. “Let’s get your make-up and hair done, then we’ll work on the outfit. I can sign you in at the club and keep you hidden until Jordan sees you."

Tears filled Crystal's eyes. She was so lucky to have family like Sierra.

"Hey…" Sierra touched her shoulder.

"Thank you. This means so much to me."

Sierra pulled Crystal into her arms and hugged her tightly. "You're my best friend and a part of my family. Now let's knock Jordan into the next century."

* * * *

Jordan glanced at his friends. Max and Damon were staring at him. "What?" he asked.

"Are you crazy? You haven't talked to her yet?" Max said.

"Even I know that's not a good sign," Damon said.

"What was I supposed to do? She said she needed some time, and I understood that. I've called." *More times than I can count.*

Max shook his head. "I don't know what to tell you except to go over to her place and talk to her."

"I can cover for you tonight," Damon said.

Jordan was about to turn him down, then changed his mind. He had let this go on too long. "Thanks. Where's Sierra? I want to ask her if she's talked to Crystal lately." Max hadn't told him when he'd asked if Sierra had talked to Crystal lately.

"She'll be here in a few minutes." Max glanced at the door, and his features froze.

Damon smiled.

"What is it?" Jordan turned, and his jaw dropped. What the hell was Crystal wearing? His heart pounded as he kept his gaze on her. She was beautiful, and it wasn't how she was dressed in the sheer skirt and top. He wanted to run to her and scoop her into his arms, but he was frozen in place.

* * * *

Crystal fought down her nerves as she and Sierra walked into the club. When she glanced around to find Jordan, she saw him with his back to her. Max and Damon had stunned looks on their faces, and her confidence level rose, until Jordan turned around.

"Go," Sierra whispered, giving her a nudge.

Crystal stumbled forward, reminding herself no matter what happened with Jordan tonight, she was free of her family's influence. Tonight she would show him she was his in the way only a sub could.

"Master Max, Master Damon." She inclined her head at them before looking directly at Jordan. "Master Jordan, Sir."

"You look great," Damon said.

"You'll turn every Dom's head tonight," Max commented.

Jordan groaned, and Crystal hoped it meant something. "Thank you both." Taking a deep breath, she dropped to her knees in front of Jordan.

His swift intake of breath was the only warning she had before he spoke. "Oh, hell no." Jordan grabbed her under the arms and lifted her to her feet. "You never have to kneel in front of me."

"But…" Her words trailed off when he glared at her.

"Excuse us." Jordan took her by the elbow and led her toward one of the secluded areas of the club.

"Jordan," she protested. "What are you doing?" Had she misjudged him?

215

"You and I are going to talk." He found two chairs, put them across from each other and pushed her down onto one. "What the hell are you wearing?" he asked as he sat down.

Their knees were touching, and the heat from his body called to her, but his question threw her for a loop. "I thought you might like it." Did he hate it? Was she fooling herself by dressing like this? Her confidence dropped.

"You're going to have every Dom in this place panting after you. Is that what you want?"

"No." She took a deep breath. "I want one person panting after me. You." It was time for her to lay all her cards on the table no matter what the outcome.

"What's changed?" His eyes narrowed in suspicion.

"Several things." She took a deep breath. "My family is history. I will no longer have any contact with them." It had been a hard decision, even once she came to the realization how toxic her family was. She found her inner strength and sent a long letter to her family, wishing them well, but telling them she would no longer be in contact.

When his expression didn't change, she fought down the sense of failure. "I'm sorry I didn't return your calls. I had to get my head on straight."

"And did you?" His tone was flat.

Wariness filled her. He wasn't acting like a man who wanted a relationship with her. Well, to hell with that. Oh to hell with all of it. If he didn't want a relationship with her, if she'd misunderstood his messages, then it was on her. "What the hell is wrong with you?" she demanded. "I come here to tell you I want to be your sub, no matter what. I want to be in your life, and yet I can feel your reluctance, your reticence." She started to rise, but Jordan put his hands on her shoulders and kept her in place.

"You left me a letter after you cleaned out your office. A letter. You asked me to give you time and space."

"I did." She took a breath. "I did, and I'm sorry for that. I should have talked to you."

"Why didn't you?"

At least he was talking to her. "Because I was scared. Scared of what I was feeling. I needed time to find myself once again." Time to convince herself she was worthy of Jordan. She was. She deserved the life she wanted and wouldn't bow to the expectations of others.

"It took you almost two weeks."

"Nine days to be exact." She lifted her chin. "I took the time for us, Jordan. If I hadn't, then I would always worry my own fears would come between us."

"Haven't I made it clear you can talk to me about anything?"

His features softened, and Crystal took a breath. "You did. But it was something I had to do on my own. Or should I say almost on my own." No holding back. "I started seeing a kink-friendly therapist."

Jordan's eyes widened.

"All those resources came in handy." She gave a little smile.

"Did it help?"

"Yes." She tilted her head. "I'm sorry if I took so long. I needed to do it for me." She straightened. "I get it. I hurt you too badly, even if I did it for the right reasons. It's—it's okay. So if you'll release me, I'll leave." It was the last thing she wanted to do, but she wouldn't guilt him into staying with her.

"I'm never letting you go."

She blinked. "What?" Her hearing couldn't be wrong…could it?

"I know you heard me."

"I'm confused." She tilted her head to stare at him. Was he saying what she thought? Her heart pounded.

"Will you tell me what you and the therapist talked about?" His hands were gentle but firm at the same time.

"Mainly my family. Their views on sex, and how I grew up." She'd cried more times through her sessions than she thought possible. "She helped me see I don't need to feel guilty about not loving my toxic family."

Jordan stayed silent, and she continued. "What it took for me to leave at eighteen was like tearing a part of myself apart. I didn't realize how much it affected me. I'd lost my family."

"So there's no chance you'll make up with your family?"

She shook her head. "My family isn't going to change. They're dysfunctional, and that's on them." She took a breath. "But it doesn't mean I have to be unhappy. I love my life here. I enjoy going out, being with my friends. I enjoy being with you and being a little kinky."

"I enjoy it too." His lips tilted up, and a ray of hope filled her.

"I had to work through what might have happened if Brady's family decided to go forward with their threats. While it might have hurt my reputation, it wasn't world-ending. My family finding out and showing up would have been world-ending. Plus, I worried about you, Max, Sierra, Damon, and others here at the club."

"We would have survived."

"I know that now. You have to remember the little girl inside of me still wanted her family's love, but their love is conditional. I deserve unconditional love."

"You do." Jordan shifted, parting his legs to pull her chair closer to him.

"Once I made the decision, the rest fell into place." Crystal lifted her chin again and looked Jordan in the eye. "I love you. I want to be with you. In and out of the club. I want to learn more about kink and explore it with you. Only you."

Jordan stilled, and Crystal's heart dropped.

"Look, if you're going to reject me, then make it quick," she said. She'd survive his rejection somehow.

Jordan threw his head back and laughed. "For that, you're going to get a spanking. For doubting me."

Crystal shook her head. "What?"

"You need to have more confidence in your Dom."

"But—"

He put his fingers against her lips.

"Yes, I was angry you left. Angry you wouldn't answer your phone or return my calls or trust me to help you through this. But seeing you tonight, in this outfit, kneeling for me and only me blew it all away." He shifted closer to her. "I love you, Crystal."

Tears filled her eyes. "Oh, Jordan," she whispered.

"I didn't know how to help you when you obviously didn't want it. I was worried you would choose your fears over us. But most of all, I didn't want to lose the love of my life."

"Never," she whispered.

"I've been dealing with some of my own shit. My father came to see me."

Crystal clasped his arm. "And I wasn't there. Oh God, I'm so sorry." Her heart hurt. "I hate I wasn't there to help you."

"I'm glad you weren't. While I'll never forgive him for killing my mother, he is my father. His blood runs in my veins. I didn't realize, until he mentioned something about his temper, how scared I was I might have the same anger within me."

"You don't have a temper," she said.

"I do, but nothing like his. When he left my office, a weight lifted from my shoulders. A part of my life was done with, and now I can move on." He framed her face with his palms. "I know how much family means to you."

"I have a family," she said. "My family is you, Sierra, Max, Damon, Tessa, and the others. We've made our own family. I'm not giving you up."

"I love you so much, you couldn't if you tried."

Crystal laughed; Jordan dragged her into his arms, and they kissed.

"This is where you belong, in my arms and in my bed."

"There's no place I'd rather be."

"Now, shall we discuss the spanking you deserve?"

* * * *

Jordan led Crystal over to a straight back chair. He sat down and then patted his legs. "Over you go."

"You were serious, Sir?"

He stared at her. "I was. You need to remember you can come to me with any problem, any issue, but especially ones that affect both of us, and we will work them out together. Now over."

Crystal sighed, and positioned herself over Jordan's legs, her feet and hands touching the floor.

Jordan ran his hand over her butt, and she shivered as he lifted her see-through skirt to reveal her thong. "For not talking to me." He brought his hand down on her ass.

A small sound left her lips, not because it hurt—yeah, there was a sting—but she knew Jordan was taking it easy on her. He would pause after four swats and rub her ass. Then start again. Her blood heated, and after a few minutes, she craved something more intense.

"More, Sir," she whispered as he helped her to her feet.

"What?"

"Please, Sir. I need something more. My body is on fire."

"Crystal, are you sure?" His eyes conveyed concern with a hint of reluctance.

"Show me more of your world. Please, Sir."

"Would you accept the touch of my flogger?"

"Oh yes, Sir." Her skin tingled with excitement.

Jordan nodded and led her over to St. Andrew's Cross station. Luckily, it was empty.

"Safe words?" he asked.

"Yellow and red, Sir."

He nodded. "Remove your skirt."

Taking a deep breath, Crystal slipped the skirt down and stepped out of it. She picked it up, folded it, and handed it to Jordan.

"Thank you, my sweet." He brushed a kiss over her lips before he placed her skirt on the table. Jordan guided her up to the cross. "I'm going to restrain your arms." He brought her arms up over her head.

The feel of his soft cuffs being clipped around her wrists caused a flood of heat to flow through her body. She turned her head, and her eyes widened: everyone in the club had gathered around.

Max held Sierra, who looked like she wanted to rush the stage. Brady leaned against Sage, who stroked his hair all the while smiling at Crystal.

"Okay, my sweet?" Jordan ran his hand over her back.

"I'm fine, Sir."

"Nothing heavy duty. Use your safe words if needed."

"I will, Sir." And his touch was gone. Crystal kept her eyes downcast toward the stage. She jumped when the tails of the flogger caressed her ass.

"It's a rabbit fur flogger. Remember when we talked about them?" Jordan's voice was soft.

"Yes, Sir. Fur on one side of the tail."

"Correct." The tails were now trailing up her back to her arm, then over her shoulders to her other arm and down her body.

The shiver that shook her body wasn't fear; it was anticipation. The first swat hit her ass. Crystal squealed and went up on her toes. But it didn't hurt. Instead, heat filled her, and her nerves tingled.

Another swat to her left ass cheek, then her right, and back to her left. She clenched her muscles with each one, not in pain but in anticipation and pleasure. It was instinctual.

"Relax, sweetie." Jordan's breath caressed her ear as he rubbed her butt. "I can feel the heat flowing off of you. Give in to the sensation. Don't tighten your muscles."

"Yes, Sir." He was right; she needed to relax.

The next swat was in a new spot on her ass, and instead of tensing up, she closed her eyes and relaxed. The next three swats made her feel like her blood was on fire. Every nerve in her body was awake and humming with need.

"So beautiful." Jordan's hand caressed her ass once again. "One more set."

The swats this time were different. More…thuddy, that was the word. They didn't hurt; there was force behind the strikes, but not so much as to make it painful.

No, the flogger caressed her skin. She didn't know how to process the sensations. Each hit took her body higher and higher. Pleasure wove its way through her veins. Her nipples were tight, and her pussy throbbed.

Then the flogger stopped. Crystal's head fell forward as she tried to catch her breath.

"You are so fucking responsive." Jordan's voice was husky as he released her arm restraints. Crystal practically fell into his arms. "Okay, sweetie?"

"Fine." She turned her head and placed a kiss on his chin. "I love you."

Jordan's grin was huge. "I love you too." He swept her into his arms and carried her into the aftercare section. "Be right back."

Crystal watched as he cleaned up the station and stored the flogger back in his bag along with her skirt. Then grabbed a blanket before returning to her.

"How did you like your first flogging?" He wrapped the blanket around her before pulling her into his arms.

"Different and I want to do it again." She grinned up at him.

****

Jordan couldn't describe the emotions flowing through him. The closest he could come was love, devotion, and happiness. Things he hadn't felt in a very long time. Crystal did that for him. She'd taken the spanking and then asked for more.

Flogging her had taken control. He hadn't planned on flogging her tonight, but when she asked, he could hear the need in her voice. Crystal's eyes lit up, and Jordan realized it was time. She was ready to take the step.

He'd given her a couple of swats with his hand before he took her to the stage with the St. Andrew's Cross. His Crystal. His arm tightened around her, and she didn't blink or express any concern.

She trusted him. It was humbling and euphoric at the same time. He was so lucky she'd come into his life.

"You were fantastic up there," he whispered.

"Thank you. I enjoyed the feel of your flogger on my skin and the way you caressed my ass as heat flowed through my body."

"For your first time, you did well. Was it as you thought it would be?"

"Once you told me to relax, yes. The sensations cascading through my body, the pleasure—not pain."

"I'm glad."

"So when can we do it again?"

Jordan laughed. "How did you feel about people

watching?"

"At first, a little nervous, but then I realized it was no different than us watching a scene. I closed my eyes and concentrated on feeling."

"Attention." Max's voice carried throughout the club. The club went quiet. "Next Saturday is Valentine's Day, and to celebrate, we'll be having a masquerade party. Better start thinking about your masks now."

The buzz that went through the club made Jordan smile. Everyone was excited. "How do you feel about coming to the party in nothing but a mask?"

"Behave." Crystal tapped his chest. "Mask, yes. Clothing, yes. It sounds like fun."

"As long as you know the only fun you'll be having is with me."

"Of course. I don't want anyone else."

"All mine." Jordan whispered as he took her lips in a kiss.

Today, tomorrow, forever.

His Crystal.

Thank you for reading Entice the second book in the Wicked Sanctuary series. If you missed Max and Sierra's story, you can find them in Tempt. Next will be Damon and Tessa's story in Seduce out in spring of 2021. If you enjoyed this book, please consider leaving a review wherever you prefer, and know that it would be greatly appreciated.

For new release information and news about Marie Tuhart, please join her newsletter via her website.

Other books by Marie Tuhart

Her Desert Prince (Desert Destiny)
Her Desert Doctor (Desert Destiny)
Her Desert Horseman (Desert Destiny)
Her Desert Protector (Desert Destiny)
Highland Dom (McMillan Passion)
Bound & Teased
Claimed by the Sheikh
Billionaire's Cowboy's Conquest
More of You (Club Crave)
Reflections of you (Club Crave)
Bound to Love You (Club Crave)
Hot for You (Club Crave)

ABOUT THE AUTHOR

Marie Tuhart lives in the beautiful Pacific Northwest. Marie loves to read and write, when she's not writing, she spends time with family, traveling and enjoying life.

Marie is a multi-published author with The Wild Rose Press, Trifecta Publishing and self-publishing. To be alerted to her new releases you can join Marie's newsletter or check out her website at www.marietuhart.com.

Seduce: A Wicked Sanctuary Novel
A preview

Prologue

"I'll take Tessa home."

Tessa Ruthledge stared at Damon, his dark hair ruffled by the slight wind. She pulled her coat tighter, refusing to consider it wasn't the chill in the air as they all stood outside the bookstore, but rather the intensity of those deep blue eyes.

Not only no, but hell no. Tessa turned to her friends. Sierra and Crystal always looked out for her. "I'll grab a cab. Don't worry about me."

"Like hell you will." His heavy male hand was on her shoulder before she could take a step.

Tessa stiffened and pinned Damon with her death glare. At least that's what the kids at the library called it when she stared at them when they got too loud.

"Listen. I'll keep my hands and opinions to myself." He lifted his hands in front of him.

Yeah, right. Tessa weighed her options. They'd all come from the monthly book club meeting at the local adult store. Normally she'd go to coffee with them, but she had an early morning meeting.

Her friends watched her. She didn't want to ruin their night, If she said no, her friends would insist on driving her home and missing time out with their boyfriends. Tessa almost grinned, boyfriends was such a vanilla term for what they were.

But alone with Damon? A tremor shook her body. Her attraction to him was something she didn't need in her life right now. Really what choice did she have? Damon was the type of man who wouldn't leave a woman alone to catch a cab or a ride share. Having him drive her home wasn't that big of a deal.

"As long as you keep your word," she said.

"I always keep my word." Damon glanced over at their friends. "She'll be safe with me."

"I believe she will," Sierra said.

"Damon will be a complete gentleman," Jordan said, glaring at Damon.

"I give you all my word. I'll drive Tessa home, see her to the door, and then I'll leave. Promise."

His words sounded sincere but there was mischief in those blue eyes. Tessa huffed out a breath. How long before he showed her he was like the other men in her life and betrayed her in some way? What the heck was she thinking? Damon wasn't going to be in her life. It was a ride home nothing more.

Tessa turned to her friends. "Friday night. At Sierra's place?" She couldn't wait for some serious girl-time to hear from Crystal about her and Jordan. The drive here with them hadn't been enough.

"Yes." Sierra piped up.

"Let's go," Tessa said to Damon. She started walking to the parking lot, leaving him to catch up with her.

"In a big hurry," Damon said jogging to her side. "Green SUV is mine."

Since there were three vehicles in the lot and she knew who the other two belong to, the green SUV was a logical choice. Tessa sighed. Logic. How often did she rely on that? Too much. She was tired of making all the decisions, yet she had to. She had no one else to rely on.

Damon unlocked the vehicle, and held the passenger door open for her. Tessa used the running board as a boost to get inside. She wasn't short by any means, but this was a luxury SUV.

The soft leather seats held her body in a soft caress. The dash board looked like something out of the space shuttle. It put her little compact car to shame. Damon climbed in. The vehicle purred to a start.

"Where do you live?" he asked.

"The apartments over on Olive."

"Nice area." He pulled out of the parking lot and turned right. "It seems like you and I keep getting off on the wrong foot. If I did something that upset you, I'm sorry."

She blinked, then turned her head. He apologized? This man, she'd only met twice, who made her feel things she thought long buried, was sorry. Tessa's insides began to thaw.

"I'm sorry too." It wasn't all his fault. "I've been stressed lately and I guess you were an easy target."

He chuckled and Tessa's nerves tingled at the sound.

"I know a great cure for stress." He flashed her a sexy grin.   "What?" She tried yoga, bubble baths, hell, even meditation. Nothing seemed to work.

"A night of passionate sex."

Tessa opened her mouth, then closed it. She'd fallen right into that one. Yet in her mind's eye she saw her body entwined with Damon's. She wasn't considering his suggestion...was she? Nope.

"Sorry, no deal."

"Come on, Tessa. We'd be good in bed together."

"We've known each other a couple of weeks, we've only been together with our friends present. Hell, we haven't even had a first date."

"All that complicates life. I'm talking one night."

She stared out the passenger window not answering him. Damn, she wanted to take him up on his offer. It had been a while since she'd been with a man, by her own choosing. Oh she'd gone out on dates, but nothing special. Nothing that made her want to bring a man home to her bed. Damon tempted her, in more ways than one. But she wasn't going to fall for his seduction routine. He probably used it on all the women he dated. Didn't all men have a line to seduce woman into their beds? She'd been burned enough.

Her apartment building came in to sight. Relief flowed through her. Damon pulled into a parking spot and she turned to him.

"Thank you for the ride. And for the offer, but no thank you." She reached for the door latch.

"Tessa." His quiet voice and hand on her arm stopped her. "I told everyone I'd walk you to the door."

"It's not necessary."

"Yes, it is." He released her and climbed out of the SUV. He helped her down, and then cupped her elbow.

Tessa pulled her keys out of her purse. The main door to the complex was unlocked, again. She'd have to call the management company, again.

"Shouldn't this be locked?" Damon asked when she pulled it open.

"Yes." She marched down the hallway to the elevator. Maybe it was time to move. She didn't want to just yet as she hadn't found the perfect house. The trip to her apartment on the fourth floor was swift. "This is me." She stopped in front of 403, she inserted the key in the dead bolt.

"Allow me." Damon pushed her hand away and turned the lock, then put the key in the door knob lock and turned. "It's better to have two keys," he said as he pushed open the door.

She rolled her eyes, but kept silent. The lamp in the living room was more than enough light to see inside.

"Stay there," Damon ordered before he disappeared inside her apartment.

What the...Tessa stepped inside her apartment. "Damon, what are you doing?"

"Making sure you're safe."

He strode out of her bedroom and down the short hall to her spare room. Tessa, hung her purse up on the hook by the door. She tapped her foot waiting for Damon to reappear. When he did, she crossed her arms over her chest.

"All clear," he said striding up to her.

"Why were you prowling around my apartment?"

"Just making sure no one else was here?" He stared at her.

"What business of that is yours?"

"You're important to Sierra and Crystal, which means you're important to Max and Jordan, which means you're important to me. It's about safety."
He kept his gaze on her. "Hasn't a man every done that for you before?"

Tessa tilted her head. "No," she whispered. Her heart melted a little bit.

"Then you've been hanging out with the wrong men." He ran a finger down her cheek. "Until we meet again, sweet Tessa."

Damon brushed past her and pulled the door shut behind him.

Tessa locked the door and let out a sigh. Maybe Damon wasn't so bad after all. Only time would tell.